The WOMAN WHO ATTRACTED MONEY

a Robert Chance mystery

STEVE CHANDLER

Robert D. Reed Publishers ● Bandon, OR

Robert D. Reed Publishers
P.O. Box 1992
Bandon, OR 97411
Phone: 541-347-9882; Fax: -9883
E-mail: 4bobreed@msn.com
Website: www.rdrpublishers.com

Editor: Kathy Chandler and Cleone Reed
Front Cover by SeeSaw Designs / Angela Hardison
Front Cover Photo:
        "La Vie En Rose" © Milena Sobieraj @ istockphoto.com
Back Cover Photo: Santa Monica Pier at night © James Price
Cover Designer: Cleone L. Reed
Book Designer: Debby Gwaltney

ISBN 13: 978-1-934759-40-0
ISBN 10: 1-934759-40-6

Library of Congress Control Number: 2009933718

Manufactured, Typeset, and Printed in the United States of America

Dedicated
to Fred Knipe

Acknowledgments

To Kathy Eimers Chandler for editing and sublime guidance; to Angela Hardison and SeeSaw Designs for cover art; to mentors Fred Knipe, Steve Hardison, Dale Dauten, Michael Neill and Darby Checketts for critical input; to James Price for Santa Monica Pier photography; to Bob and Cleone Reed for more publishing excellence; and especially to Sergeant Sy Ray of the criminal investigations unit of the Gilbert Police Department and the Phoenix Training Council.

Commit a crime, and the earth is made of glass. Commit a crime, and it seems as if a coat of snow fell on the ground, such as reveals in the woods the track of every partridge and fox and squirrel and mole.

Ralph Waldo Emerson

I smile when I'm angry.
I cheat and I lie.
I do what I have to do
to get by.
But I know what is wrong,
and I know what is right.
And I'd die for the truth
in my secret life.

Leonard Cohen

1

Robert Chance rolled his office chair up to the computer screen that still held the devastating email he received yesterday. It was the email that informed him of Tom Dumar's death. No matter how many times he read it, he felt it.

Like a kick in the stomach.

So sad to have to tell you that Tom took his own life.

He thought back on his last coaching session with Tom. He had seemed very angry, but strong. Nothing at all suggesting a death wish. Nothing suggesting suicide.

Chance wanted to go walk by the ocean and put all the pieces together in his mind. He wanted solitude, silence and space — the three places he always went to solve problems.

Because up until now, Chance had considered Tom to be his most successful and most coachable client.

It didn't help his focus that another client was due to arrive in twenty minutes. Chance walked slowly from his office to the front hall and back. Time to pull himself together and relax enough to be a good coach to Madison Kerr. Coaching had always been a positive experience for Chance until now. His decision to get out of law enforcement and into coaching had, for years, felt like a good decision. But now?

Chance looked out the window of his home office in Santa Monica and watched the wind blow a hummingbird away from the feeder, but the little creature just circled back onto the other side.

Life.

Don't we usually fight for it?

What kind of peace can suicide really give a person? Suicide is over so fast. You barely have time to appreciate its effects. And there's no second-guessing the decision.

Chance's wild thoughts were fortunately distracted by Angie, the golden dog who couldn't stop staring up at him. Angie always knew when something wasn't right. Chance stroked the top of her head. "It's okay, Angie. This is the way of the world. It doesn't have to make sense immediately."

Angie wagged her tail at the sound of her name.

"But it will have to make sense soon, because when I worked with Tom in our last session he was filled with a stubborn kind of hope. Like you, Angie. Filled with hope."

Angie got up and walked into the next room, satisfied that her master was okay.

Chance went into his kitchen to brew a pot of coffee for himself and Madison. He did some arm stretching exercises in front of the coffee maker as it sputtered and hissed. Then he went to the open window and did some relaxed deep breathing from his heels to the top of his skull.

He poured himself a cup.

Chock Full O' Nuts. Heavenly coffee. Well, maybe he didn't like the coffee itself as much as he liked its name and history... how they hired Jackie Robinson as a spokesman. How they changed their jingle's line from "better coffee a millionaire's money can't buy" to "better coffee a billionaire's money can't buy" to keep up with the times.

Everything's an expanding story, thought Chance. So how did Tom Dumar's story contract and collapse so fast without me seeing it coming?

Can you have suicide and heavenly coffee at the same time? Chance's mind felt out of control. After stirring in some thick cream he lifted his cup to the window, to the hummingbird outside, as in a toast.

Here's to the profession of helping others.

Here's to those who still want help... no, let's just say, here's to those who still want to live.

2

Madison Kerr definitely wanted to live.

She wanted to taste life at its deepest levels and not miss a thing.

She shook Chance's hand firmly and walked into his office and sat in the comfortable stuffed chair he had bought for his clients to sit in at an estate auction in Sacramento.

She was dressed for business with a white blouse, a black sweater, and a charcoal grey skirt that stopped at the knee. Her thick dark hair was brushed out and she wore a double-strung pearl necklace, an outfit that may have been subconsciously designed to strike a nostalgic chord with her older clients earlier that day.

"Hello Robert," she said. She paused. "You heard about Tom Dumar."

"Yes."

"You were coaching him, weren't you?"

"Yes I was."

"Do they think it was suicide?"

"Yes they do. Did you know Tom?"

"I knew a lot of people who knew him. I'd met him but I didn't know him that well."

"Very sad thing," said Chance. "But what can you and I work on today that would most help you in your life?"

Madison Kerr sighed and looked out the window. Grey gulls coming in from the ocean were gliding above Chance's lemon tree. Chance's seaside Santa Monica home always intrigued her because she couldn't figure out how he became this wealthy. A former cop doesn't usually live in a place like this. She'd have to get the whole story someday later. Right now she was too excited about the work they were doing on her career.

She pulled a small journal from her purse on the floor and uncapped her pen. She liked the coaching sessions, and especially liked spending an hour with her notes later that same evening. She looked back up from the notebook to Chance.

"I still can't seem to make my business work," she said. "I mean, I'm very busy and I'm making a lot of connections and friends, but there's so little cash flow. I keep listening to my CDs on attracting abundance, but nothing seems to be happening."

Chance let his mind turn over the word abundance. He thought of his parents and how they worked so hard to make ends meet. Was abundance a word they ever spoke? Ever even considered? Maybe it came with the flower child generation. Summer of love. We deserve it all.

"Let's start right there," Chance said, sitting up straight in his office chair, assuming his most optimistic get-to-work position.

Madison shifted in her chair as well. "Okay," she said. "Start right where?"

"Attracting abundance," he said. "Does that have a clear meaning to you?"

"What do you mean?"

"If you were to begin attracting abundance right now, as you were sitting here, would either of us know that you were doing it?"

"I don't know. Are you saying it's not a good thing to do?"

"Well...maybe not... not if we don't even know what it is."

"Can you talk more about that, because I always thought... well, I don't know what I thought."

Chance opened his spiral notebook. He wished he hadn't because he came to the page where he'd recorded his post-coaching notes with Tom Dumar. No notes about depression or despondency. Just an excited, charged-up guy. He quickly turned pages to a blank area and wrote today's date and Madison's name.

Chance spoke carefully, "People can only do what they can see themselves doing. They live into their clearest and simplest pictures."

"Okay. So I'm not being simple enough," said Madison.

"You're business may not be."

"I thought having a good education and a good intellect meant that you entered a more complicated world."

"It doesn't have to work that way. You can keep it simple."

"So what would it mean for me to have a simpler picture?"

Chance sat back in his chair and relaxed. He said, "If the house is on fire, you picture yourself getting out the bedroom window, and immediately you are standing in your back yard. It's immediate and efficient."

"Okay."

"That's much different from listening to CDs about home safety."

"The abundance CDs are very peaceful."

"I bet they are. Probably better than a sleeping pill. But you say your challenge right now is making money."

Madison certainly agreed with that. She could put in long, busy days and still find her business struggling at the end of the week. "How would I create a simple picture for myself?"

Chance shifted in his chair. He remembered his own life changing when he understood this. So he wanted to proceed carefully. He said, "What if, instead of trying to attract abundance, you were simply earning money?"

"That would be great."

"So. Just know that you can cause it to happen. Rather than the law of attraction, we want to try on the law of cause and effect. Much more effective."

"Try it on?"

"Right. Just try it on, like you would a jacket."

Madison smiled and said nothing. She was writing notes. She put the cap back on her pen. "Now may I ask you something?" she said.

"Yes."

"Are you hurting right now? I mean, to be a coach and to have a client die like Tom died and then to have people tell you it's suicide, it has to be the hardest thing for you to hear. It must feel like devastation for you."

Chance looked at Madison for a moment and let the beginning of a small burning in his eyes disappear.

He knew she was right.

He did worry about taking Tom's suicide personally, like a blow to his ego as a coach. If he was coaching Tom's life and Tom couldn't bear to live any longer, how good a coach could he be? How good a friend, even? But he brushed these thoughts away quickly.

He knew from his police days that too often a suicide victim's friends and relatives wanted to personalize the tragedy. Make it be about them. What did I do wrong? What could I have done? This is *my* loss!

Then he looked at Madison and said, "Let's hold our focus today. Let's have this be about you."

He got up and walked to the window and sat on the ledge. Madison could see that his back was almost bending the stalk of a potted rubber tree plant, but she didn't say anything because when Chance was animated, the physical world seemed to leave his awareness.

Madison watched him and said, "Okay, what about the law of attraction?"

"It's a little like the law of gravity," said Chance. "It's a real law, but the point is how are you going to use it? Just because you understand the law of gravity doesn't mean you can now fly a plane."

"How do we know I'm not using the law of attraction successfully?"

"I don't know. Maybe look at your bank account."

Madison was writing things down and Chance let her finish. She finally looked up as Chance said, "What if you became a woman who produces income? Instead of a woman who is trying to attract abundance. Can you feel the difference?"

"I'm feeling it already, but I'm also feeling some fear."

"Yes, I know, because you go into new territory using that language. Even just to think it. You are looking straight at reality. Looking reality in the eye. Who's going to blink?"

"That would be me. I think I'm blinking."

Madison started writing the new phrases in her notebook as Chance walked back from the window around his desk and settled into his chair across from hers. He watched her finish her notes. She looked back up with a hint of excitement in her eyes.

"I think this is a good start for me," Madison said.

"Yes, I think it is," said Chance.

"Can we slow down and go back to some of these money-making phrases so I can tell you the fear I feel when I think about them?"

"Of course. That's what we want to do."

"Is it crazy? That I feel all this fear about money?"

"No," said Chance. "It's very common. It's the norm. And I can really relate. Any fear you feel, multiply that by ten and you have what I was like. Long ago, but still unforgettable."

"That's hard to picture."

"Very true, though. I could tell you some stories."

"What did you do to change?"

"Exactly what you and I are doing."

"Which is?"

"Become more accurate. Get real. Remove the fear."

Madison sat in silence. Then she said, "Now, can I say something unrelated?"

"You can always say whatever you want... you know that."

"I think I know who killed Tom Dumar."

 **3**

Chance stared at Madison, wondering what to do with her last comment. He leaned back in his chair. How could *she* know who killed Tom Dumar? And who said he was killed? After taking a long, slow breath he said, "Let's save that for later."

"You aren't interested? He was your client."

"I'm *very* interested, but right now I'm coaching *you*, and you are my agenda; and unless Tom's death is something you need coaching on, we will continue working with your thoughts about making money."

"Versus attracting it."

"Exactly."

As the session continued, Chance kept bringing Madison back to her fears about money and finances and her desire to mystify the process and somehow force it into a vague "spiritual" dimension.

Chance said, "Your whole *life* can be spiritual. And you can also earn money by selling your services. That's how life can work when it fits together without fear. You're *in* the world but not *of* it. As the masters say."

"Right. The masters. It's a couple weeks away, and I think Phil might beat Tiger this year."

Chance smiled. There was something about Madison that he liked in a way he couldn't put words to. Something about the depth of her outlook on life. It was innocently irreverent.

Madison Kerr had set up her private consulting business to help people make money on the internet. Her previous career was in advertising. That career had been disrupted twice when the agencies she was working for failed to keep up with her own progressive marketing techniques. They lost clients when their radio, TV, and newspaper ads failed to work. Madison was frustrated. Rather than join yet another agency and try to talk *them* into internet communication, Madison finally decided to start her own business and do it herself. She was good at it and she liked it. She had hoped the money would follow, but with some rare exceptions, it had not.

As the coaching session ended Madison and Chance confirmed the date and time of their next meeting; and as she stood to leave, she gave him a friendly hug.

Chance said, "I may be calling you later about Tom Dumar. Of course I am interested in what happened... what you might know."

"Thank you for staying with me... the subject of me, today. I really love how focused you are, no matter what else is going on."

"It's just simpler that way. But thank you."

"I know, you keep saying that. About making things simple. Every time I try to tell you how much I admire your integrity or your honor and loyalty, you talk about just keeping it simple."

"That's all it is. I appreciate your compliments, but it's related to what we worked on for you today. The simpler the better. The simpler things are for you, the more powerful you become."

Madison nodded her head toward a frame on Chance's wall. It was an album cover of Charles Mingus the jazz bass player. The album was autographed by Mingus (Chance bought it in an estate auction), and below it had a card Chance had made up with Mingus's words in quotes:

Creativity is more than just being different.
Anybody can play weird; that's easy. What's hard
is to be as simple as Bach. Making the simple
awesomely simple, that's creativity.

Chance smiled and looked admiringly at the framed album cover. The album was titled *Better Get It in Your Soul.* He gave a thumbs-up sign to the album and then to Madison, "Have a great week! Keep it simple. Get it in your soul."

Madison laughed and closed the door and walked down the cobbled steps to her four-year-old mint green Volvo which always looked brand new. Chance watched her through his front screen door and allowed his thoughts to return to the death of his client and friend Tom Dumar.

4

Madison's comment kept returning to him all day: *I think I know who killed Tom Dumar.*

Chance guessed that Madison had been reading the local papers about the multitude of real estate projects that Tom was trying to extricate himself from. Many of Chance's coaching sessions with Tom focused on how to exit dysfunctional agreements—and how to do it with grace and honesty. One of the sticking points for Tom was that there wasn't always integrity on the other side of the table recently, especially with his former partner Glen Gibbon.

Was Gibbon the man Madison thought was behind the death of Tom? That would be the gossip column speculation, and Madison usually wasn't interested in gossip. It sounded as if she knew something more tangible. He made a decision to call Madison later that day for a non-coaching conversation. He hadn't wanted to bring it up at the end of the coaching session because clients need to process the work they do, especially in the hour that immediately follows a session.

Chance grabbed his cell phone and punched in Madison Kerr's number. She answered immediately.

"That was quick," she said. "Is this your post-session client courtesy call?"

Madison was the kind of woman who was flirting no matter what she said, Chance realized. Or maybe it was him, and how he heard her. Was she too attractive for her own good?

He settled down.

"Madison, we need to talk about Tom. In the office I let what you said go, but there's a feeling I have about this, and I think I need to know what you know… or think you know."

"I'm free at 8:30 tonight after my dance class. How about the Koi Pond at the Fairmont? The Fairmont Miramar Hotel on Ocean Avenue and Wilshire? They serve food and drinks outside."

"Okay, I'll be there. Do you think you've got something more than speculation about Tom? I know his lawsuits and battles with Glen Gibbon were all over the news."

"I do. What I have is simple and precise. Just the way you like it."

"Till then," said Chance who closed his phone and plugged it into the recharger on the wall so he wouldn't be tempted to use it again.

5

Chance's thoughts eventually returned to Susan Dumar, Tom's wife. How do you talk to someone whose husband has just died by his own hand? Are there books of advice on this?

Maybe you just do it.

Whenever tragic moments like this occurred, Chance preferred to stumble right in. Take some small immediate action. Do it wrong if you have to, but do it. Fail forward. Don't worry about how you're coming across, *because it's not about you.*

So Chance opened his phone and called the newly widowed Susan and reached her on her cell.

"I am so sorry," he said. "I don't know what to say. How are you right now, Susan?"

"Okay, I guess," said Susan. "I'm just rather numb. Robert, how could this have happened? He was so happy about the work he was doing with you. He saw so much freedom in his future, and he was almost out of his real estate deals altogether... it just doesn't make any sense. Can you come over? You're one of the few..."

Chance knew he was one of the few people who really knew Tom. He had been coaching Tom for a year now. Some people called it life coaching, although Chance never liked that term for it. Especially now. Life implies a living person.

Of course, Susan, I'm on my way." Chance looked down and saw his retriever Angie looking up at him. "I'll just feed Angie and I'll be there. Who's with you now?"

"No one now. Everyone else left to deal with the mortuary and all that. I can't make myself participate in that. Suicide. It's just so strange. The thoughts you have. The amazing guilt...."

"Yes, and are you sure... well, was it certain that..."

"Oh, it's suicide, all right. We'll talk when you get here."

Chance said goodbye and put away his phone.

He opened a can of meat and organic vegetable mix for Angie and scooped the moist food into her dish. Angie could sense that Chance was leaving, having heard him transfer his car keys to the slacks he'd put on; and she quickly lost interest in the food and went to the front door, obviously wanting a ride-along. Her nails scratched the front hall cobblestone in anticipation.

"Not this time," said Chance to the golden dog. "This isn't exactly a joy ride today."

Chance slipped into his faded old ivory-colored MG and eased it out onto the highway that ran along the Pacific Ocean, on his way to Laurel Canyon. His CD player started playing Brad Meldau's moody piano version of *Dear Prudence*, but Chance quickly shut it off. No distractions, he thought. Too much to think about. And Meldau's piano always led his mind away from the real world. How did Meldau do it? How did he keep it so simple and yet so surprising?

It was heroic.

It was how Chance himself wanted to live.

He rolled down the window on the driver's side. The breeze off the ocean felt humid and good. Reassuring. He mentally went back over his last two coaching sessions with his now-departed client. The wind blew across his face. His eyes began to water.

How in the world could he have not detected Tom Dumar's desire to die?

6

Had Robert Chance simply been a life coach driving to meet with his deceased client's wife he never would have noticed that he was being followed by another car.

But he had spent eleven years as a cop—criminal investigator with the LAPD—and had logged many a mile tailing cars himself. It felt surreal to be on the *other* end of a tail.

When the light turned green at Wilshire, Chance did not accelerate.

He did not do a thing.

He just sat there with his foot resting gently on the brake pedal of his car.

Cars behind him began honking and one driver was leaning out his window yelling at him, and soon Chance got out of his car and threw up his arms in a gesture of hopelessness, signaling a possible dead engine. It was a dead engine that happened to still be quietly running. But the other cars couldn't know that. Soon the cars behind him circled around him to continue through the traffic light leaving Chance's tail car exposed in an embarrassing position, not knowing whether to move forward or get the hell out of sight.

Chance was walking toward the ice blue Taurus, memorizing the pudgy face and short-cropped red hair of the young man behind the wheel when the car made a rapid, awkward and squealing U-turn. *Your second mistake,* thought Chance, because the license plate was now revealed. Chance wrote the number down on the palm of his hand as the car disappeared. *You can run,* he thought—but you will never be able to hide. Not from me.

Chance walked back to his MG, vaulted into the driver's seat, and roared off.

Far too interesting, he decided. This whole situation has become far too interesting. Simple tragedy might have worked better in his life. This was beginning to feel like the complicated criminal world he thought he'd left behind.

He cruised up to Crescent Heights Boulevard and then down into Laurel Canyon where Tom and Susan Dumar lived. Life was never simply tragic, he realized. There's always something there that is trying to reveal a bigger, better mystery. He felt a little flurry of butterflies in his stomach. Go toward it, he thought. Whenever there's fear, go toward the fear, because it wants to show you something.

He drove down into the canyon.

7

Susan Dumar had short black hair and big brown eyes that made people think of Betty Boop or Katie Holmes, depending on how old they were. Her big eyes were red today as she opened the big cabin door and motioned for Chance to come in.

"I'm glad you're here," said Susan, taking Chance by the hand and leading him into the living room where they both sat on a long couch covered with a red and green striped Navajo blanket. "Do you want coffee or tea?"

"I'm fine," said Chance, "and how are you right now?"

"Just shell shocked."

"Will it help to talk?"

"Yes, I think so. They found Tom in his office in West Hollywood. You've been there. Melrose Avenue in the design district?"

"I've been there, yes. Was it an overdose?"

"No it was a gun. The police and detectives said it was suicide and there was an email to me."

"And the email confirmed it? It was clear to you?"

"Yes, I think so."

"Why do you hesitate?"

"No, it was definitely a last goodbye."

Chance squeezed her hand. He said, "Had he been particularly upset?"

"Well, no! You know that better than anyone. He'd completely turned the corner. He was facing everything. We were both so happy; we didn't care anymore about money or investments; we were willing to sell this house and rent a place and start life over. I feel strange, like he's still here. I keep trying to talk to him. When do I start the stages?"

"Stages?"

"You know, the four stages of grief."

"Optional, of course," said Chance.

"Oh, so I don't have to grieve?"

"I'm not going to tell you what you have to do Susan; I'm just here for you whatever you choose to do. People just assume they have to go through horrible things, like stages of grief, and in my experience they don't really. But I understand fully."

"Everything's a choice to you, isn't it?"

"Yes it is."

"Tom used to tell me about that after his coaching sessions with you. We would sit up for hours."

"Tom was getting some real strength back in his life," said Chance. "Why do you believe he would do this?"

"I suppose the dealings with Glen Gibbon had been more stressful than he admitted," she said. "Gibbon was such a pig, don't you think? And I feel so guilty. Where wasn't I there for him that he would do this?"

"You were there for him."

"So what can I do now? I feel so helpless. At least we don't have children, but still. If you were coaching me, what would you say? My doctor says I should take some prescription he gave me to calm me down, but I hate those things, and why should I go into a medicated fog? To postpone what I really feel?"

"Doctors write prescriptions for anything. I go into the office, my doctor asks how I'm doing; I say I'm not too happy about the Dodgers' losing streak, and he pulls out a prescription pad. Anti-depressants. Doctors now believe you shouldn't be feeling anything."

"Their pharmaceutical friends have convinced them of that," Susan said.

"Exactly right." Chance smiled at her. "Humorous world we live in."

"Except for now. It has lost some of its humor. It's just so hard to face the truth of this."

"I'd say that the truth is usually better than what we imagine," said Chance.

"How do you mean that?"

"Our minds seem to go to the worst places first."

"Are there better places to go when someone dies? I want to go there. I want to turn the clock back and *do* something. I want to help Tom right now. And I know I can't anymore."

Chance put his arm around Susan's shoulder. He saw a box of Kleenex on the polished redwood coffee table and handed the box to Susan. "If you really want to do something right now, you can help me," said Chance.

"Are you in one of the stages?"

"No, I am looking for truth — the real thing — not everybody's opinion. Do you want to look with me? And you don't have to. I'll respect whatever you want right now."

"I want to look with you."

Chance looked at Susan. He was impressed by her strength in this situation. Tom had always said she was a strong partner.

"Good," said Chance. He took her hand again. "Please show me the email. His last email to you."

Susan began to shake slightly and cry. Chance moved closer to her on the couch and held her again. He took part of the Navajo blanket and put it around her shoulders. The wind in the canyon felt like it was coming under the door, and it was cold and sad and bleak inside. The largest and oldest eucalyptus tree in the world hung over the cabin and cast tumbling, rotating shadows in through the windows. A fire in the granite fireplace across the room was about to go out. Chance got up slowly and walked over to add a small log to the fire. He then added a larger log and began to stoke the fire with a brass poker. When he turned to tell Susan he would be glad to come back another day, he saw that she had left the room. Chance heard the tiny blips and beeps of a computer connecting up in a back room.

25

As he looked back into the fire he saw a single stream of orange and blue flame forming a shimmering spiral around the two new logs. If we light this tragic situation up, he thought, and go for the whole truth, will it really be better than letting it all fade away?

He knew the answer was yes.

The truth was always better than what the human mind usually wanted: unconsciousness. Head in the sand. Hiding away. Avoidance of reality. That would not happen in this case. The truth would be sought and found. And that truth, whatever it was, was something he wanted to give to Susan.

Susan came back into the room with a piece of paper in her hand. She folded it over and sat back down on the couch. She motioned toward the fire where Chance was still squatting like a baseball catcher with the poker in his hand.

"Thanks for that," she said. "Mustn't let the fire go out. That was always Tom's thing. He'd start the fire and then seem to be hypnotized by it. He was very internal, wouldn't you say? Very thoughtful."

"Very. May I ask you a strange question?"

"My favorite kind."

"What in the name of all that's sacred is a death coach?" said Chance. "I just noticed this piece of paper here in the kindling basket and it says 'Death Coach' on it. Not that I'm nosy."

"Oh that!" Susan shook her head. "I was looking on the internet to find out about the stages of grief and I saw that there was this guy who calls himself a death coach. He helps people who have lost loved ones, I guess?"

"I've never heard of it, but it doesn't surprise me. However, it's not the most comforting name."

"He turned out to be rather nice."

"You called him?"

"I was open to anything. His prices were a little high."

"What do death coaches charge these days?"

Chance and Susan had a hard time keeping straight faces now. There was something about this line of questioning that had become absurd, and it felt welcome. After they both

27

laughed, Susan unfolded the paper she had printed out from the computer and handed it to Chance.

Chance read it twice:

Susan. I am sorry for this. This will be better for you and I. I was in deeper than I realized. You are better off without me.
Tom.

Chance looked up at Susan. She was searching Chance's eyes. Chance didn't know what to say, and then he said it.

"You know he didn't write this," said Chance.

Susan just stared at him. She looked like she was five years old, ready to hear the world explained to her. Chance came to the couch and put his arm around her shoulders.

"Tom was a civilized man," he said. "He knew the English language. He never would have said 'This will be better for you and I.' You know that, Susan."

"It's 'for you and me,' right? And he was not ungrammatical."

"No, he was not."

"It's just too terrifying to let that in. That he didn't write this to me. But are you sure? Doesn't suicidal thinking make you... he might have taken drugs, or been drinking...?"

"It doesn't make you suddenly ungrammatical, no. There are other things about this note that don't feel right, either."

"So what does this mean?"

"It means I'm going to need your help because I'm not going to just let this go. Tom would not have wanted that. He'd developed a pretty strong sense of fair play, as you know, and..."

"Is this Gibbon?"

"Wherever the truth is. That's where we're going."

"And you used to do this? You were police, right?"

"Yes I used to do things like this. We'll find the truth."

"What's next to do?"

"Do you have the keys to his office?"

"Yes."

"That's what's next. I'd like to go there now and see what I can find. Do you want to go with me?"

"I should stay here for the family," Susan said. "So you go. And, about the four stages of grieving."

"What about them?"

"Is revenge one of them?"

"No. And neither is justice. But that doesn't mean we won't go there."

"Why did the police say it was so definite, open-and-shut suicide?"

"I don't know. They made a rare mistake?"

Susan could see that Chance was being sarcastic. In fact, Chance had experienced too many of his colleagues on the police force who were less than thorough in their work. They were just there for the paycheck. Whatever got them through the day with the least amount of hassle.

Add to that the fact that law enforcement in California had been repeatedly messed with by political operatives who had no respect for it. Social engineers trying to level the landscape into an amorphous terrain where nothing was right and nothing was wrong. Where only power was left. Or, at least the illusion of power.

Real power, for Chance, was always found in the simplest truth.

Chance stood to leave as Susan went to a desk by the window to get Tom's extra set of office keys. Through the window Chance could see the final streaks of sun piercing the dusty brown and forest green glory of Laurel Canyon. One half expected to see Hansel and Gretel running through the dry leaves chased by a witch. How many stories can this enchanted forest handle?

Chance took the keys and said, "Susan, for now one thing is very important. Do not sign off on a cremation."

"The family wanted that; they wanted to scatter...."

"No scattering, Susan. There must be nothing scattered,

okay? Not right now. We must hold together for a while. For Tom. And for you."

"For Tom and me."

"Grammatically correct. You've got it. Hey. Tom's eloquent use of language just might lead us to the truth."

"The truth. Which stage of grieving is the truth?"

"The truth knows no grieving. It's what sets us free."

9

The Koi Pond at the Fairmont Hotel had a few white metal tables and chairs for outside diners, and by this time at night it was chilly enough to have only Chance sitting there. He was early for his meeting with Madison and wanted extra time to think and make notes.

Why would someone want to follow him in a car? A simple suicide case wouldn't cause that to happen, but this was just not looking like a suicide.

The writer of the email who put "better for you and I" probably mocked his English teacher when he was young. Didn't need to study. He knew enough of the language to get what he wanted in life. Get. *That's the key word*, thought Chance, *get*. Get. It was always behind everything that went wrong.

What was someone trying to get?

Chance made notes on a yellow pad. He drew circles and put Tom Dumar's name in one and Glen Gibbon's name in another. He put the word "suicide" in a third circle and started drawing meaningless lines connecting them all. He underlined Gibbon's name. Gibbon was the one Tom Dumar was having trouble disconnecting from. Their mutual real estate investments had come undone and Gibbon was playing hardball. Tom had just wanted out.

A waitress came by Chance's table for a second time.

"Coffee, with cream," said Chance. "And I'll be expecting one more person." Chance had always had his coffee black until a long visit to England last year convinced him that cream was a good thing.

Chance stared at the huge goldfish in the pond next to his table. She said it was a koi pond. Were koi actually goldfish? He'd want to Google that later. He watched the orange fish circle around the green-spotted rocks and olive-colored seaweed. He wondered if fish experienced anything resembling greed. Or grief. A soft hand rested on his shoulder. Madison was early.

"Have you been waiting long?" she said.

"No, I got here early to think things through a bit," said Chance, standing up. "Big questions. Like whether koi are goldfish or a different kind of fish altogether. They sure look like goldfish to me."

Madison was wearing a bulky turquoise and grey-flecked sweater over her black dance class warm-ups, and her eyes were as blue as the Pacific Ocean sky had been earlier in the day.

"What have you figured out?" Madison said.

"About the fish?"

"No, about Tom."

"That the suicide was probably not a suicide, and that's about as far as I've gotten."

"I told you that earlier."

"Yes you did."

"You didn't believe me?"

"I didn't *not* believe you. I just put your remark on the back burner."

Madison motioned for the waitress and ordered a glass of red wine.

"I did some business for Glen Gibbon once," she said to Chance. "In an old ad agency of mine. He was a nightmare to work with and our account team started calling him Monkey Mind."

"A gibbon is a kind of monkey isn't it?" said Chance.

"Yes. It is."

"Why was he a nightmare to work with?"

"He always smiled when he was angry. For starters. And he

was a frugal miser to the point of near insanity. Plus he was a top figure in his church and was always talking to us about how he knew that what his church taught was true. Yet his real religion was money. He was obsessed. He tried to cheat us and short us on everything. He thought he was a great negotiator. He was really proud of himself. But he was just an evil man. Dressed up in his religion."

"Interesting. Now tell me what you don't like about him."

Madison laughed and picked up the menu. Chance picked his up, too. It was long past dinner time and neither of them had eaten and the items on the menu were starting to look good.

"Do you want dinner?" said Chance.

"Yes."

"Good. I do, too. The pan-seared orange tuna here is supposed to be quite good."

"It is, indeed," said Madison.

Chance had forgotten that Madison knew everything about Santa Monica. He himself didn't care much about restaurants and nightspots. Give him a few good books and coffee with cream and his evenings were complete. He could live anywhere. But Madison and Santa Monica went together.

Madison set her menu down. "It turned out that Gibbon was worse than a hypocrite," she said. "He started cheating the agency out of its billings and refusing to pay what he owed us. He'd always claim some technicality, some error we had made. He'd try to get refunds."

"Okay, but I'm not seeing where any of that makes him a murderer. Are you basing your suspicions on just that? He was a miser and a cheat with money? I pretty much knew that. I'd been coaching Tom on how to remove himself from all the partnership real estate deals he'd had with Gibbon, so I knew about the 'frugal' side of Gibbon. The deals were almost finished. Gibbon had no motive to get rid of Tom that I can see right now."

Madison shrugged and started to speak again but the waitress stepped up to the table to take their orders. Both ordered the tuna — Chance with white beans and Madison with steamed broccoli. After the menus were taken away, Madison sipped her wine and looked at Chance.

She said, "Gibbon was obsessed with Tom's wife."

"Susan?"

"Susan."

"Isn't Glen Gibbon married with about eleven children?"

"Right. Actually only two kids."

"By obsessed, what do you mean?"

"Pictures of her on his computer. Video of her walking out of her cabin. He's even had people followed who visited her or called her or knew her."

"People followed? How do you know this?"

"I went into his computer. I told you I was advanced in that field — that I was always a little ahead of my time. I was hacking before I could talk."

"Well, yes I knew that, but I didn't know you were a criminal, Madison."

"That's a technicality. He'd already stolen so much from us that I waived my own adherence to the letter of the law. I wanted to go after him. That's when I discovered his obsession with Susan Dumar."

Chance stirred his coffee and shook his head.

Madison said, "May I ask you something?"

"Madison, we're not in a session right now. You can just talk. Like a regular person."

"When you stop coaching people, what happens?"

"What do you mean?"

"Do you ever talk to them again? See them? Are you friends? Or, what?"

"It depends. Some former clients have become good friends. Some I lose touch with. Or only hear from once in a while. Why do you ask?"

"I'm just thinking." Madison took a piece of olive bread from the basket and took a small bite. "Do you think our coaching will work for me?"

"You mean teach you to attract money?"

"Teach me to *make* money."

"Yes, I do."

"I do, too," she said. "I think it's already working. But I wonder, then what?"

Chance put some powdered sugar substitute into his coffee. He didn't know exactly why he did that because he never used it. He wanted to steer the subject in a new direction. "Do you remember our first session?" he said. "Or maybe it was our second. Where we did the whole session on the subject of the future?"

"Yes! How could I forget! It was when you showed me how all my anxiety came from worrying about the future."

"Well. That's it then. There you go."

"And that the present moment was everything. The present moment was eternity in disguise, where everything gets created. Even the future."

"You're good."

"I take notes."

The waitress arrived balancing two plates and Chance made room on the small table for their dinners, looking forward to bringing the conversation back to Tom Dumar and Glen Gibbon. There was a small splash in the koi pond and both Chance and Madison turned to look. Some of the koi were bright orange, and some were white with orange spots. Chance asked Madison if she thought they were big goldfish or a different species altogether.

"Do you know what a homophone is?" Madison said.

"Is it different from any other kind of phone?" Chance said.

"That's very funny. But the word is homophone and it refers to the English language."

"I guess I forgot."

"It's a word that sounds the same as another word, but is spelled differently and means something entirely different — like the words carat as in diamonds, and carrot as in vegetable. When you hear me speak them, you don't know which one I'm saying."

"Oh yes, thanks. This has been a grammar appreciation day for me."

"And so *koi* is Japanese for carp, but it also is a homophone for another Japanese word, also pronounced koi," said Madison.

"What does the other word mean?"

"Love and affection," she smiled.

Chance sighed a big sigh, grabbed his yellow pad and made room for it on the table. He set his half-finished tuna on the table behind him and pulled out his pen. "Now tell me everything, no detail too small... everything you found out about Glen Gibbon when you visited his computer," Chance said.

● ● ● 10 ● ● ●

As Madison began to pull her laptop from her gym bag, a chilly Pacific Ocean breeze swept in under the palm trees over the pond and made them both involuntarily shudder. Chance was wearing a faded brown polo shirt and thin khaki slacks, and they were no longer comfortable.

"Let's go inside," he said. "Let's try to focus. There's a fairly private corner in the lobby we can go to for the moment."

Chance left cash in the little black folder containing their bill for dinner. They gathered their things and saw that the elegant Fairmont lobby was almost entirely empty except for one very tiny elderly couple checking in. They went to a corner coffee table and set up there. Madison got her laptop going and looked up at Chance.

"Gibbon was obsessed with Susan Dumar," she said.

"So you said. Did he do anything to act on it?"

"I can't tell from what I found on his computer."

"Did she know about it?"

"Doesn't look like it. Why don't you ask her? You know her, right? I never found anything that suggested it wasn't just a one-sided thing, though. Just pictures of her...and strange emails from some guy who talked about visiting her in Laurel Canyon."

"This was all out in the open on his computer? What if Gibbon's wife or kids...?"

"Oh no," Madison laughed. "He hid his data steganographically."

"Oh that clears it up."

"Don't you know what I mean?"

"Sorry if I'm not cyber-obsessive."

"Which is to say that you are a dinosaur?"

"Yes."

"Don't get me wrong. I love dinosaurs. Barney is so much fun to watch."

"What is data hidden steganographically?"

"Well, it means he just hid his Susan Dumar stuff inside another file. You might have seen this technique used on the internet to hide a picture inside of an audio clip, for instance, but it can also be used to hide larger amounts of data. You can create an encrypted disk of any size inside of an inconspicuous-looking file."

"Well of course you can."

"So you knew."

"Actually I'm lost, but I trust you."

"I mean, you don't have to know *how* to do all this, Robert, to understand the information it gives us."

"Which is what I'm saying. So Gibbon had a crush on Susan."

"That's a quaint way of putting it. Very flattering to the stalker when you talk like that."

"But murder? How does that follow? Especially if she was unaware of his attentions. If this was a kind of distant platonic... hobby."

Madison closed her laptop. She looked at Chance for a long time and said, "It's just a knowing, an intuition I have."

"I'll need something more precise."

"Yes, I know that about you."

● ● ● 11 ● ● ●

Chance patted his pants pocket as he drove into West Hollywood to make sure the keys to Tom Dumar's office were there. This would be a difficult visit, he thought, given that his coaching career had removed him from this sort of clandestine crime scene activity for a few years now.

He parked on a street two blocks away from Dumar's four-story office building and locked his car. He walked along slowly, like a man out for a stroll. The front of Tom's building had pale green panels inside squares of aluminum strips, more appropriate for a medical clinic than a real estate office building, thought Chance, but hey it's California, where nothing is predictable.

What was he going to be looking for when he got to the fourth floor where the office was? Chance didn't know. He would be very interested in finding out why the police were so sure this was a no-brainer suicide, and maybe the office where Dumar was found would show him something.

Getting off the elevator at the fourth floor, he verified that he was alone in the building. It was after eleven, so that didn't surprise him.

Chance got to Dumar's office and as he opened the door, he began looking for any signs of forced entry. He entered the office slowly and checked the windows and doors around the office for any signs that someone had broken in to get to Tom.

There were none.

He turned on the overhead fluorescent lights and saw an office that looked and smelled like it was recently scrubbed clean. The smell of ammonia was so strong his eyes began to water. There was no chair behind the desk, so that had to have been removed. And now he could smell other disinfectants everywhere. Chance looked in the corner for where Dumar's computer had been and there was nothing.

For a simple, sad suicide, someone had gone to extraordinary lengths to remove things. He saw a fragment of yellow and black police tape on the corner of the desk. Chance found nothing in the large drawers. He spotted Tom's faded red and gold University of Southern California wastepaper basket in the far corner of the room. He glanced out the window at the Hollywood night lights and then crouched down to look through the trash in the basket.

But there was no trash.

Just a single business card. He turned it over and saw the gold LAPD seal on it and the name Detective Anton Mossi. Criminal Investigations. Must have been the guy who confirmed the suicide, thought Chance. Mossi. Somehow the name felt familiar.

Then it came to him. Tony Mossi had crossed paths with him years ago when that little girl had disappeared from the playground at Beverly Hills Middle School. After two months of frustration and no results from the police, Chance was hired by the girl's grandfather to find her. He found her in less than twenty-four hours. She was safe and sound in Apache Junction, Arizona, living with her father's sister. And Mossi had called him to chew him out for interfering. It was not a pleasant exchange, and it was obvious that Mossi's ego had been wounded.

Chance had asked Mossi why professional competitiveness would take priority over the safe return of a young girl, and Mossi had flown into a rage. As Chance stared at the card it all came back. And now, even the odd act of leaving his card in the wastepaper basket seemed like ego to Chance. Perhaps it was resentment of the University of Southern California, the school of privilege and status? Take that, smart-assed college guy... you're dead and I'm the cop that gets to say how.

Chance knew there would be an unpleasant visit tomorrow to the LAPD so that Detective Mossi could educate him on the telltale signs of an obvious suicide.

● ● ● 12 ● ● ●

Mossi's office was small with dingy blinds whose openings redistributed the early morning California sun streaks that had already lost strength fighting through the clouds coming in from the ocean.

Chance had worried that the detective might not agree to see him, but then he realized that an ego like Mossi's can never leave well enough alone. If there remained an uncomfortable sense of having been bettered by Chance's investigative skills, then Mossi would want to keep the issue alive until Chance was put in his place. Real cops didn't have a lot of respect for private investigators. And although Chance had been a cop before, the finding of the lost girl was on a private contract.

Chance entered Mossi's office and closed the door behind him, still holding a styrofoam cup of untouched lukewarm coffee given to him by the receptionist in the outer office.

Mossi leaned back in his reclining chair behind his desk and motioned to Chance to sit.

"Are you coming out of retirement and looking to get back into the force?" said Mossi with a wary half smile. "Because I heard you were not doing law enforcement work anymore."

"This is nothing official, detective; just following up on the death of a friend, Tom Dumar."

"Oh yes. Sad deal. Suicide. In his office. An Airweight snubnose .38 Special revolver. Very unpleasant gun to fire."

"Right. Especially if you have never fired one before. Even more unpleasant if you have never even seen such a gun."

"Meaning what?"

"Meaning I don't think Tom killed himself. I know he didn't own a gun, because he was my client and we talked about things like that."

"Client? I thought you had given up snooping around. Aren't you some sort of consultant?"

"Life coaching."

Mossi let out a howling laugh.

"Of all the phony baloney fake professions that we're so proud of here in California, that one takes the cake," said Mossi. "What, people don't know how to live? They need a coach for that? What are your credentials? I bet you don't even need a license to do it."

"No, it's not therapy. It's just coaching. That's why they call it coaching."

"Just another racket in my book. For people who don't want to take the time to get a degree in psychology."

"It differs greatly from psychotherapy, detective."

"In what way?"

"You have to get results."

"Oh, well, congratulations on Tom Dumar then. Because the *result* of your so-called life coaching is that the dude is dead. Not exactly the result you were after."

"You're right about that."

"So now you want me to save your ego, pull your chestnuts out of the fire, by helping to prove that he didn't kill himself? Trust me, Chance. I'm a professional. I carry a license. He killed himself. How else can I help you?"

"Will you share with me the factors that led you to conclude that?"

"I will not. Anything else?"

"If I told you what I had so far, would you be interested?"

"Not unless it blew me away. What do you have?"

Chance hesitated to explain how the email with the ungrammatical "This will be better for you and I" was probably not written by Tom Dumar and after he had laid it out to Mossi he realized that it was not going to impress him.

A smiling Detective Mossi said, "You people, you intellectuals, you USC types, you think you live in such an elevated world, so far above the rest of us."

"I'm University of Detroit, myself," said Chance.

"Whatever. Doesn't matter. Just let real cops handle the real world and you go do your life enhancement work or whatever it is that can't seem to even keep your clients breathing."

"You're still a little upset over the Covington girl."

"I don't know what you're referring to... oh okay, *that* mess? That's known as the Blind Pig Case around here because you found an acorn after we had done all the footwork."

"Right."

"Look, Chance, I'm not in the mood to do you any favors. I know your reputation. They say you were the best investigator and the best interrogator we ever had. You could talk the birds out of the trees. In some ways I'm kind of in awe of you, I'll admit that. But until you've got something more substantial than something only an English teacher would understand, I'm not opening anything up here. I've got enough real world crime to deal with. Are we through?"

"For now."

"Okay, then, good luck with your life coaching. If you were really good at life coaching you could coach some life back into your deceased client. Now *that* would get you some business. You could call yourself The Lazarus Agency."

"You're not a very happy man, are you Detective?"

"Maybe just not when you're around. You left the department rather abruptly, didn't you? Left me here to live up to your reputation, and I have not appreciated that. There's a lot of mythology around you."

Chance smiled and winked at Mossi as he left his office. He had a feeling he would be back. And he didn't mind it at all that Mossi had raised the bar on finding proof that Tom didn't kill himself. Chance always welcomed an outside challenge that would get his inside bar raised, too.

 **13**

Madison Kerr sat on a large towel on the beach just fifty yards from the Santa Monica Pier, in a blue tank top and torn white cutoffs with ragged white frilly threads that made her legs look tan. The sun felt good until it felt like a hot flash and prompted her to run into the waves to cool herself off.

She knew her real goal should be to obtain internet consulting clients right now and make some real money, but she couldn't let go of her investigation of Glen Gibbon. She was convinced that Gibbon was tied up somehow in Tom Dumar's death, and she felt a strange thrill probing his computer files from her laptop.

What was Gibbon's fascination with Tom Dumar's wife about?

Madison closed her eyes and felt the sun go behind a cloud as she recalled all the Susan Dumar voyeuristic materials she had found. Her mind then turned to the email exchange between Gibbon and someone at a wildlife association in Laurel Canyon. Gibbon had asked for information about eucalyptus trees. How strange. Why was this in his hidden Susan Dumar files?

The association's email to Gibbon was in response to his questions about recent fires in Laurel Canyon. They told him that the eucalyptus trees were very flammable, and that they pose other problems as well. They have shallow root systems and will easily topple over in strong winds, crushing houses, cars, utility lines, and people. The association had declared the eucalyptus a public nuisance.

Madison pulled out her cell phone and punched in Chance's phone number and was happy to hear him answer on the first ring.

"Robert, it's Madison. Can you talk for a second?"

"Sure."

"May I come in a half hour early for our session today?"

"No, that won't work. We could do an extra half an hour at the end of the session. Would that accomplish the same thing?"

"Yes."

"Is it about Gibbon?"

"Yes, I've found some curious things. Inside the Susan Dumar file he has put an email exchange about eucalyptus trees."

Chance said nothing.

Madison said, "Did you hear me?"

"I don't see what that would be," said Chance. "Maybe this is a file of his favorite things. You know, raindrops on roses, whiskers on kittens, eucalyptus trees, Susan Dumar...."

"I think this is more serious than that. If you won't take this death seriously, what, hypothetically, would be serious to you?"

"Let me think for a minute."

"Never mind. I'll talk to you about this after our session."

"See you then."

Madison folded her phone and put it into her bag. She toweled herself off and collected her things. She felt the damp sand under her feet as she folded her towel and put everything in her over-sized burlap bag. The bag had a blue sequin outline of Minnie Mouse on it. There was something about this investigative work that she loved. Was that sick?

She couldn't put her finger on it.

Was it because it brought her closer to Robert Chance?

Maybe.

Was it because it allowed her a way to go after Monkey Mind Gibbon? That wasn't it.

It was something about the work itself. The adventure and the hunt. She'd always wanted to be more than just a businesswoman. At one time she remembered she even wanted to be Xena. She remembered as a teenager how she loved watching Xena on TV. What did they call her? A warrior princess! Could there be any better job title than that? A warrior princess is what she wanted to be.

Somehow this work, this hunt, made her feel like that. It just felt good. Did it have to be a *secret* desire? She made a decision to bring this subject up in the coaching session.

Chance had told her once that we were as sick as our secrets. So she didn't want any more secrets.

14

Chance had made it back to his home office in time to put hot water on for tea. Madison Kerr liked coffee in the morning and tea in the afternoon. Chance liked to take time to prepare for his clients' coaching sessions. It was almost a Zen ritual for him. Often in the preparation he received visions of his clients' futures.

Gentle visions, but visions all the same.

When Madison was seated with her chamomile tea and honey, Chance asked if he could share just such a vision.

"Oh absolutely," said Madison, cradling her too-hot cup and blowing on the surface.

"Too hot? I thought you liked it hot."

"I used to, but I just read a study. Drinking scalding tea can lead to esophageal cancer. So I'm going to let it cool from now on."

"Glad you're keeping up with the latest studies. It will all change in a month or two, all the health advice, but it's fun to know what to be scared of now. Fear can be trendy."

"Knowledge is power," she said. "So what do you learn from your visions?"

"I see you loving the whole process of investigation," said Chance. "Not the old paradigm. Not Mickey Spillane or the old private eye stuff. But the future. Into the cyber world. Your world. It's the future of the field. And I just see you being great at it and enjoying it."

"That's visionary?"

"Is it wrong?"

"Well, no."

"You can see it, too?"

"Yes, I wanted to talk to you about it! As I was doing the research on Gibbon, I got this feeling. I don't know how to describe it. It's just exciting when I do it. More than my other work. What is it?"

"Maybe it's called a calling. When you get a feeling like that, maybe you are being called."

"That doesn't sound like you. I thought you were Mister Specific No Nonsense Action Man, and now we are talking about a calling?"

"We are."

"Okay. I like it that we are."

Madison let a small smile play across her face. She half-closed her eyes. She couldn't remember ever being this relaxed. Finally she said, almost in a whisper, "When I was a little girl my most exciting time was doing the little puzzles in my kids magazines. As I grew older I loved going to the library. When everyone else hated research papers, I was in heaven. Tracking down information that others couldn't find."

Chance listened. He set down his coffee cup and said, "Do what you love and the money will follow. I know that's a worn-out old saying, but sayings become worn out because of the truth in them."

"But how do I earn a living going to the library?"

"That's what we're here to find out. And you know that the library's online now."

"I do know that. I think I know that better than you know that."

"I agree with you on that."

"But what about specific ways to earn money?"

"We will get there but we have to start with what you love."

"But this sounds mystical," said Madison.

"No, that's just it," said Chance. "It's not. It's logical. Let's challenge it."

"Okay, if I love what I'm doing… why does that attract money?"

"There you go with the attraction again. You keep wanting to be a woman who attracts money, but I want you to see that you can *produce* it. Much better that way. Puts the power in *you*, not in the money."

"I can feel that."

"So, what really happens when you love doing something?"

"When I love something I can do it all night long."

She blushed and quickly added, "I mean I lose track of time when I'm doing it."

"And the good thing about that is?"

"Money wise?"

"Yes, sure."

"I do more of it. I do it with more energy. I don't look for ways to interrupt myself. I don't put it off."

Chanced stood up and went to the window. He straightened out a bamboo stalk in a pot on the ledge and put his finger in the black rocks to see if they were moist. They were not. He turned back to Madison.

"I think you're on to it now," he said. "Think of it this way. If you were designing a robot, and you wanted the robot to be productive, wouldn't you make it focused and unswerving? You wouldn't design a robot that was a distracted clock-watcher would you?"

"No," said Madison. "No. I'd design a focused robot."

"If you wanted maximum productivity."

"Exactly."

"And what's mystical about that?" said Chance.

"Okay. You have convinced me. I'll become a librarian now and make a fortune because we know they do." She gave him a playful look.

"Or an investigator," he said.

"Like Nancy Drew?"

"I'm betting she was your favorite."

"She was. Until I graduated to Agatha Christie," said Madison

"At the age of four, I'm guessing," Chance said.

"Fourteen, but close enough. After that it was Jane Tennison."

"Who?"

"Helen Mirren's character in *Prime Suspect*."

Chance smiled and walked back to his chair. He pointed at Madison's teacup and she put a hand over it and said, "No thanks. But how do I start? I mean, how do I get into investigation?"

"You tell me," said Chance.

"Maybe I start by looking into the suicide case of Tom Dumar."

"That's one idea."

"Aren't the police already way ahead of me on that one?"

"Unfortunately not. I met with the lead detective on the case, a guy named Mossi, and to him there *is* no case. So they are not ahead of you."

"But what happens to my other business if I jump into this full out? What happens to my cash flow?"

"As we've worked on before, you have to ask for what you need. Most people could have anything they wanted in life if they would just ask for it. And then keep asking."

"Then I would ask for a retainer to cover my work looking into this case."

"Perfect."

"But who would I ask?"

"Who wants it solved?" said Chance. "Always find out who needs or wants what you have to offer."

"Is everything a teaching moment for you? Doesn't a conversation ever just go where it goes?"

"We are in a session right now," said Chance. "I am coaching you. So I won't let moments go by. Who wants this case solved?"

Madison thought for a while.

"You do," she said.

"You're right, I do."
"You would pay me a retainer?"
"You would have to ask."
"Will you pay me a retainer?"
"My checkbook's right here in my desk. Let's get started."

 **15**

Chance walked along the beach by the Pier in Santa Monica. He could hear shouts from teens on the Ferris wheel, and a drifting melody from a street singer singing the John Prine song "Hello In There." He pictured a pile of dollars and coins in the gold velvet of his open guitar case. Making money now, versus attracting it in the future. Works every time.

The gulls made their ridiculous squawking noises as he began his walk down the beach away from the pier. He imagined that the gulls were sounding alerts to each other about possible fish below the surface of the Pacific as the waves ripped in and out.

The sand closest to the water was damp and firm, and that's where Chance liked to walk, so the ground beneath him wouldn't give way with every step. He wondered if he could have been a gull in a past life. Looking for fish below the ocean surface of life. Looking for clues to a mystery. Was he now looking for more than that? Was he also looking to avenge his friend? Or to comfort his own ego? What would it matter if he were?

Life was too short to be sure of everything.

What was he really after? Chance's mind strayed to the word *closure*. He didn't like the word. He never understood why the families of crime victims needed some kind of final courtroom circus act to give them closure. They didn't feel complete… couldn't even get on with their lives, until the criminal's trial was over?

What if there was no trial, as is often the case? What if they let the killer free? That happens too. Why do people need other people's official pronouncement and judgments to allow themselves closure? Why couldn't they just close everything themselves, their own way? That's why Chance loved his coaching work... he could help his clients not have their emotional lives be at the mercy of other people's pronouncements.

Chance saw a gleam of metal in the wet sand and squatted down to pull it out. It was a quarter. He thought of how excited he'd have been as a small boy finding this. But now? They had to change the Chock Full O' Nuts jingle from millionaire to billionaire. He walked on. He brushed the sand from the coin and slipped it into is back pocket. I'll donate this somewhere, he thought. Keep it circulating.

Maybe it would come back in the form of a small clue.

Clues were the coin of the realm to his mind right now. Nothing like being on a case. It gave life dimension. It picked up the pace. He began to breathe more deeply. It felt good. Every breath you take. Every move you make. I'll be watching you.

Madison wasn't like him. She actually liked terms like *closure* and *validation*, borrowed from the world of psychotherapy. Chance did not. He saw them as watchwords and buzzwords for inside access to a manufactured sacred circle. Such phrases exist, also, in cults and fraternal organizations, the more secret the better.

We are as sick as our secrets.

As he looked at the beautiful homes in the distance along the southern California shoreline, he thought back to the Charles Manson murders. Talk about sick secrets. Crazy Charlie was a cult leader living nearby in the desert with a killer team of devotees. Manson's many days and nights on LSD and worse led him to believe that the Beatles' *White Album* contained secret messages directed personally at Manson. Manson was especially titillated by the song "Helter Skelter," which he interpreted to be a call for him to participate in an apocalyptic race war in America.

There's reality, and then there's the story we add to it.

And there's no limit to how bizarre a story can get.

In Chance's mind this all related to the secret meaning people had given to the spooky terms "closure" and "validation." How was achieving closure better than finding the truth?

Walking like this always opened Chance's mind. Something about the left side of the body balancing with the right side of the brain, and vice versa, that led the mind to open up and see new patterns... the mind now becoming a reverse marionette. Even though this left-right mind-opening was a theory long held by Chance, he was beginning to read research by neurosurgeons and scientists working with stroke victims that proved that the body *could* bring back the brain.

He'd already known that for a while now. It was drummed into him during every workout he had with his martial arts trainer Wu Li.

In fact Wu Li himself was often called into the UCLA Medical Center to help work a partially paralyzed stroke victim's limbs with weights, and push them hard, so that the opposite half of the brain would come back. The old work ethic wins again, thought Chance. We used to simply coddle the stroke victim. And because of that their health got worse.

In his cop days Chance used to walk to solve cases. Now he walked to see his coaching clients' problems more clearly. Amazing the insights that would pop up on a walk. Right brain, left. Left brain, right. The feet and the brain calling each other home. As the mind expands and rises up it gets a great bird's eye look at the truth.

And he just wanted to see the truth.

Chance looked at a diving gull and thought, "We have the same job."

Chance took in the beauty of the gull's diving flight that finished with a squawk and a splash. Diving into the water and trying, always, to catch something interesting. Something to nourish the soul.

As he walked further along the beach the word "eucalyptus" came to his mind. Why was that subject in Gibbon's file on Susan Dumar?

Chance pictured the huge eucalyptus that hovered above the Dumar cabin. Most flammable tree in the canyon, he thought. So what? We aren't investigating arson here; we are looking at a possible murder.

Chance decided that it was time that he visit Glen Gibbon.

16

Gibbon was not an easy person to reach. But after a number of calls, Chance and Gibbon decided to sit down together at the Guernica Café at the edge of Muscle Beach. The restaurant was very dark, and faded Picasso prints were on the walls.

Chance and Gibbon's booth sat beneath a metallic-blue Picasso painting called "Cat and Crab on the Beach."

Chance ordered coffee with cream and Gibbon asked for lemonade. Gibbon's curly grey and brown hair was clipped short and his puffy face reminded Chance of the character in the Michelin tire ads. Gibbon was wearing a sea-green and pink Hawaiian shirt. He stirred an extra packet of sugar into his lemonade and smiled a practiced smile.

"What can I do ya for?" he said.

Chance always hated that phrase. What can I do ya for? It was fake country slang. It was a trailer park endearment. He took a minute to answer.

"It's about Tom Dumar. I know that you and he were partners in some real estate ventures."

"Tragic," said Gibbon. "I never saw that coming. I had my differences with Tom, but I never thought he'd end his life that way."

"How did you think he'd end it?"

Gibbon stopped and squinted. "Are you being funny now? Because in our faith it's a sin to kill yourself."

"That's pretty harsh."

"You're not a religious man, are you Mr. Chance? Or can I call you Robert?"

"You can call me Chance. And I don't think my religion, which I'm quite happy with, is the issue here. I think the issue is Tom and whether he killed himself, and I am here to see if you can help me understand his last days."

Gibbon drank from his lemonade and grinned. Chance remembered that Madison said he smiled when he was angry and Chance could feel it.

"*Whether* he killed himself?" Gibbon said. "What do you mean... oh, oh let me remember... oh okay I remember, you were a police sergeant once, right? Before consulting? Joseph Wambaugh kind of thing? You used to snoop around, looking into people's private lives for clues? And you couldn't get enough of that, so now it's maybe not a suicide?"

"How well did you know Tom's wife Susan?"

"Saw a picture of her once I think. That's it."

"Do you know who took the picture?"

"Who... I don't know what you're driving at," Gibbon said. "Tom was difficult to deal with. He tried to get out of all his agreements with me."

"Those agreements weren't fair to Tom. You took financial advantage of him."

"An agreement is an agreement. That's what I believe."

"No matter how unfair."

"Still an agreement. And those judgments are for others," said Gibbon.

"So you can be religious but not ethical or moral."

Gibbon smiled again. It was clear he was angry. "You know, Chance, I thought you were going to try to make me feel like I drove Tom to kill himself when I wondered why you wanted this meeting today. But this is even weirder. I know that you were his shrink, so you have more knowledge of Tom's thoughts than I ever would."

"Coach," said Chance. "I was coaching him."

"Right, and it made my life hell, if you want to know the truth, because you made Tom too big for his britches."

"Tom gained his own strength in dealing with you. I didn't make him anything."

"Well you're not going to get any kind of inside scoop from me because I'm immune from all this stuff. By the time Tom ended his life, we had ended our relationship. All our deals were settled."

"By a mediator. That guy from The Agreement House."

"Right," said Gibbon, "because that was Tom's way of getting *out* of his agreements."

"The mediator didn't think the agreements had any ethical validity."

Gibbon smiled again and opened his hands and held an exasperated pose.

"There you go again," he said. "Funny how people of little true faith get all in a huff about ethics and morals."

"We think they're important."

"You flatter yourself, Chance, and I don't like any of the lines of your questioning, so why don't we just call it a day and have our attorneys talk if there's anything else to be discussed."

"Fair enough," said Chance. He finished his coffee and stood to leave. Both men walked outside into a hazy, humid L.A. day. Gibbon walked across the parking lot and got into a light blue Taurus and Chance noted the plate. It was the same car that followed him. Different driver.

Chance walked quickly to the car as Gibbon rolled down the driver's window.

"Now what?" said Gibbon.

"This your car?"

"What does it matter?"

"Who else drives this car?"

"I'm through with you. Like I said."

"Oh, I don't think so."

Gibbon drove away as Chance stood in the café parking lot letting the puzzle pieces try to settle in his mind.

17

Chance's sister, Nikki, was gay. Or at least that's what he always thought until his last conversation with her.

"It's lesbian," she said. "It's gay to the general public, because they can tolerate that word better. But among those of us girls who qualify, we don't use the word gay that much. That's more for men."

"Okay, I didn't know," said Chance. "As usual. So how am I to keep track of this stuff, Nik?" He had called her "Nik" since she was two years old.

"Just do your best, and I'll help along the way. I think you do just fine. Most people had a hard time coming out to their families and you were the easy part for me."

Nikki and Chance were sitting in the patio of her cottage house just ten blocks inland from Chance's seaside home office. She was drinking mint tea but always kept coffee and plenty of real cream for when her big brother dropped by.

Nikki had trained to be a Methodist minister and attended seminary school in Chicago before coming back to California to be a social worker. She worked in a homeless shelter in south L.A. and wrote poetry on the side. Little literary magazines published her work.

Chance often visited her when he had lost his way.

"I have a dilemma right now, Nik, that I think you might help me with."

Nikki held her hand out to stop him talking, and then got up to turn her music system down. Her outside speakers were playing Jennifer Warnes' *Famous Blue Raincoat* album, and she didn't need the distraction right now. Chance's dilemmas were usually bigger than those of other people.

"Okay," she said and sat back down. "Tell me."

"You studied to be a priest."

"Minister."

"The Bible and all the orthodoxy."

"Yes."

"Can I ask about it? I'm trying to understand religion right now."

"Of course."

"There's a saying, 'Let there be light,'" Chance said. "God said that."

"Yes. So the story goes."

"But according to the Bible, he *then* made the sun and moon and stars. After he said that. After he made light. How is that possible? Where did the first light come from? How could there be day and night, as the Bible says there was, *before* he made the sun?"

"The Bible is an oral history passed down from imperfect man to imperfect man and then later written out by even more imperfect people," Nikki said.

"Yet some think it's the literal word of God."

"Some do."

"You don't?"

"I see it as inspired. I also get my inspiration from it. Every day."

Chance moved his lawn chair out of the direct sunlight.

"I'm trying to understand a super religious guy who seems to have no moral standards," he said.

"Are you coaching him?"

"Thank God, no."

"Thank God. How easily we thank God, even while questioning him. You're not back into investigations are you? Tell me the truth."

"In a way…"

"I thought your coaching work was going so well."

"It is, Nik. It's just that one of my clients committed suicide and I can't figure out why."

Nikki nodded and added half a packet of Splenda to her mint tea. She picked up a bowl of blue taco chips and offered them to her brother.

"No thanks," said Chance. "You deal with a lot of down-and-out people. Don't you? I want to know how they get that way. What makes a person not want to live?"

"It's about the meaning of life," she said. "They don't feel like their life has any meaning anymore."

"That doesn't seem like Tom to me, though. Seems like the opposite. It seems like Tom had some of that meaningless life when I started with him, but he kept changing and gathering strength."

"I believe it."

"But when you yourself have suicidal people that you're working with, what do you do to bring them back from there?"

"Well it's all about making a difference," said Nikki. "If your life makes no difference it has no meaning. So I try to guide people to their ability to make a difference. Let them experience that a little at a time. Let them help somebody else. Once they see they can make a difference, suicidal ideas seem to fade away."

Chance picked up a cinnamon stick and started to stir his coffee with it and then decided not to. He laid it down on a napkin.

"My client Tom had stepped up to all his unfinished business," he said. "He'd cleaned up all his bad agreements. He began helping people find property again. He was making a difference. He was feeling good."

"You have that effect on people."

"Not if they kill themselves, I don't."

"How sure are you that he did?"

Chance looked up and allowed a spark to flash across his eyes.

"I'm not sure at all," he said.

"And I knew that."

"How did you know that?"

"You had your detective face on when you came here today."

18

Madison pulled into Chance's driveway fifteen minutes early for her appointment on Friday afternoon. She closed her eyes and reclined the driver's seat back to allow for a little meditation prior to her session. She thought back on how negative her life had become prior to meeting Robert Chance.

How full of worry it was.

When her former client, the trial attorney Mariano Javier, suggested she talk to Chance, she was skeptical. How would a coach help her find the motivation to grow her business and be excited about doing so?

When Chance first invited her to his office to talk, she told him about how her life had filled up with worries. And the joy of living wasn't really there. And there was so much stress now over not making enough money, which was why she had purchased her audio program for attracting abundance.

"Tell me about the worries," Chance had said.

"I have a number of them."

"Can we write them down?"

She watched as Chance walked to a curtained window in his office that turned out to be a white board. He pushed the curtains back and turned to Madison with a smile.

"I promise this will be fun."

"Really?" said Madison. "Worries can be fun?"

"Yes indeed. We're going to take them one at a time and upgrade them."

"How do you upgrade a worry?"

"You change it to a concern."

"What's the difference?"

"There's a big difference. Concerns are higher up the ladder of consciousness, and concerns lead to action."

"I suppose I'll just trust that."

"Well, let's test it," said Chance. "Tell me your first worry. The one that puts the most pressure on your life right now."

"My mother. She's not doing very well. She has some problems with her spine and she fell a few weeks ago, and I worry about her a lot."

"Okay, that's a good one. Now, let's look at what the worrying actually does," said Chance. "First of all, how does it affect *you*? Mentally and physically."

"It has a bad effect on me. I feel stressed and sometimes just depressed. I have a hard time focusing on my work."

"So it isn't helping you."

"I guess not."

"What about your mother? How does your worrying affect your mother?"

Madison said nothing for a while. Chance waited and then put the marker down and returned to his chair.

He said, "Your mother knows you worry?"

"Oh yes."

"Does she like it that you worry?"

"No."

"How do you know?"

"One night she fell and couldn't get up," said Madison. "And she just lay there until morning. Until she could see that there was light outside before she called me. Because she didn't want me to worry."

"Anything else?"

"Yes. She had been seeing this total quack. Some guy she read about in her alternative newspaper. She was trying to get treatments for her lower back problems, and I didn't even know about it for about half a year."

"Because she didn't want you to worry."

"Exactly."

"So worrying about your mother isn't a benefit to your mother, either. It even sounds like worrying about your mother is having a negative effect on her life."

"It is! It's causing her to hide things from me. It's causing her to feel bad about being sick."

Chance gave her time to think this over. Then he said, "I don't see a lot of benefit here. Why don't we look at an upgrade in thinking?"

"Like what?"

"Like not being worried anymore, but being concerned. It's very different."

"In what way?"

"First of all, does it sound different? To you? To be concerned rather than to be worried?"

"Yes, I suppose it does. Concerned sounds less hopeless."

"That's it exactly," said Chance. "That's it. When you are concerned you are not hopeless. You're not really troubled, and you are not helpless either. You're just concerned. When you're concerned you are still in charge and you are ready to act on your concern."

"Like finding her another doctor."

"Right. If I'm concerned about my mother, I might call around to find a better doctor. Notice how concern leads to action. I was concerned about my health, so I joined a health club. Action follows concern. That's why we always—and I mean *always* – want to upgrade worry. The minute we feel it."

"And you can do that every time?"

"Yes. With practice, yes. And soon you could tell your mother that you do not worry about her at all."

"Actually she would like that."

"Yes, she would. It would take all the guilt and pressure away from her. Now she would be freer to ask for help. Parents don't want their children to worry about them."

"Okay. But isn't worry an expression of love?"

"Not at all. No. Worry is dysfunctional. It is an expression of your *own* problems, your own personal breakdown. It's not love."

"Concern is closer to love?"

"Yes, because when you're concerned you can do more to help her. That's true love. True love doesn't show up as pain. True love always shows up as love. Love looks like love when you see it. It acts the part."

"Love acts the part?"

"It certainly does. Why wouldn't it? Love wouldn't act like depression or worry. It would act like love. This is always so hard for people to see. People want their pain to be evidence of love. It isn't."

"It's hard for me to see, but I'm starting to."

Chance and Madison went through four more of her worries that day and upgraded them to concerns and then to action plans. She knew after that meeting that if they never achieved anything else, having the worry in her life now become optional was worth having met him.

● ● ●

Madison's fifteen minutes of meditation was coming to a close and she dropped the sun visor down and slid open the mirror to check her appearance one last time. She couldn't define most of the feelings she felt prior to her sessions with him, but she knew none of them were unpleasant.

She walked up to his door and realized that she was looking forward to the time they'd booked after the session to talk about her research on Glen Gibbon. She especially wanted to talk more about Gibbon's emails to the Laurel Canyon wildlife group about the flammable foliage there. Tom and Susan Dumar lived in that canyon, and Madison was surer than ever that there was more to Tom's death than a simple suicide.

As she and Chance sat down to do their coaching session, they had no way of knowing about the fire that was now raging. But if they had looked out of Chance's side bedroom window they would have seen signs of it.

They would have seen the black smoke rising above the tallest redwood and sequoia in the canyon.

● ● ● 19 ● ● ●

Madison and Chance were sitting in his office, and the focus was on Madison's love of research and expertise on the internet… and how to convert a love for that work into a real career that served people and brought in a good wage. Like a grown-up would do.

At the end of the session Madison said, "When I think about doing things in an adult, mature, grown-up way, what does that say about me?"

"What do you mean?" said Chance.

"Why wouldn't that just come naturally? What's wrong with me that I am not there yet? Why, when it comes to money, am I like a little girl?"

Chance turned his chair so that he wasn't sitting in the shaft of sun coming through the front window.

"We all start at square one," he said. "No one has ever skipped a stage in growing up. And most people get stuck somewhere along the way and stay stuck. You are not unique. There is nothing wrong with you. When a flower grows, there is nothing wrong with any of the early stages of growth."

Madison smiled. "What kind of flower do you see me as?"

"What kind of flower?" Chance was stumped. He usually never got stumped, but this time he was just blank. He finally said, "You know, we've actually run out of session time for now," said Chance. "We've entered our time for talking about what you have found on our friend, Gibbon."

Madison sighed and reached into her bag for a different notebook and pulled it out and opened it.

"I found something else last night in his PC," she said.

"First, can I ask you about that? About his PC?"

"Sure."

"Why can't he just delete anything incriminating or overly personal?"

"He has," said Madison.

"Well, then how could you ever find it? And how could we use it in court?"

"When you delete something you don't actually delete it. You have simply made the disk space inaccessible and overwritable. But until it is actually overwritten, it can be recovered by someone with the right tools. Or the right know-how."

"Someone like you."

"Exactly."

"So what if you yourself had something you wanted thoroughly deleted on your computer? What would you do?"

"If I wanted to more thoroughly destroy my data without destroying my hard disk, I'd want to perform a 'zero fill.'"

"Which is what?"

"You overwrite a pattern of zeroes over all the bits in the hard disk."

"I knew that."

"Are you being sarcastic?"

"No, I'm just in a state of admiration here. I think I must have left police investigation just in time. I can't imagine learning a whole new dimension of life like this."

"We all start at square one," said Madison. "Some people get stuck along the way and stay stuck. Others just team up with someone like me. A much smarter way to go."

"What else have you found that's interesting in the Gibbon files?"

"Not a lot. Unless you count hiring someone to commit arson."

"Are you sure?"

"All signs point there."

20

"Too early to think of arson" the newscasters were reporting as Madison Kerr sat on her bed watching reports break in from the L.A. TV newsrooms. Her laptop was open as she raced through what she had saved from Gibbon's emails asking about "catalyzing an act of nature."

Something was out of control, she thought. Something was moving faster than her new investigator's skills could keep up with. She tried Chance again on her cell and this time he answered. His voice could barely be heard above the noise.

"I'm at the edge of this thing, right at the edge of the canyon," he said. "It's too early to call it arson, but why don't you and I call it arson just for the sake of speed."

"I'm in," said Madison. "Have you been able to reach Susan Dumar?"

"Not yet. I've tried her number every few minutes and it goes right to voice mail. It doesn't look good from where I'm standing. It looks like the Dumar cabin is right in the center of the activity down below."

"Call me when you know more? I'm trying to trace some of his emails about encouraging an act of nature to happen. I'll let you know what I get."

Chance clapped the phone shut and stared at the diminishing smoke trails in the sky. The sun was beginning to set and a breeze blew in triggering an idea. He called Madison's number again.

"Me again," said Chance. "Can you get me coordinates for Gibbon's home residence? I'm going to follow up on the fact that his car followed me, even though he himself didn't."

"When was that?"

"Right before I visited Susan Dumar I was followed. I got the license number and it was the same car he was in when we met at the Guernica Café."

"You never told me that."

"You hadn't been retained."

Madison blushed with a happiness she knew she would have to dampen down if this was to proceed professionally.

"He's at 1222 North Magenta Way; major crossroads are Main and Rosebud in North Hollywood."

"I'm on my way there."

"It must be frustrating not to be able to reach Susan. Do you think she's okay?"

"We will find out," said Chance.

The fire itself had died down considerably by the time Chance arrived at the entrance to the canyon. Firefighters' lines kept onlookers out, and media helicopters had already swooped in to replace the water-dropping choppers that had left the airspace. The media was now hovering above the billowing tunnels of curled black and brown smoke.

Chance recognized one of the fire investigators from his department days, Tommy Martinez, and asked him about the situation. Martinez broke into a big grin when he saw Chance standing by his car.

"Hey, Chance, my man, when are you coming back to help us fight the forces of evil?"

"It may be sooner than you think. What does this look like here?"

"Off the record?"

"Of course. Just your gut."

"Not your typical house fire. It didn't start in one room and spread outward."

"What was it?"

"Just guessing? A blast set in that kitchen area, the part of the cabin that looks like it was an add-on under the eucalyptus."

"Leaky gas line?"

"No. It wasn't consistent with an accident. Not at all. When we called the canine crew in, they found accelerants inside and out."

"You gotta love the fire dogs."

"We do."

The two men stared back at the fire. Chance said, "I may give you a call" and Martinez gave him a thumbs up. Chance got back into his car and eased it out onto the road.

Chance usually didn't like using his phone while driving. It wasn't exactly a safety issue. He actually believed safety increased for him when he drove and talked because he was hyper vigilant when doing so. It was a matter of contemplation. He liked to drive and think, allowing his mind to work things through while he was at the wheel. He let the left side of his brain handle the mechanics of driving which freed up the right brain to find harmonies in the chaos.

This drive was an exception because things were moving too quickly for the luxury of deep thought. He called Detective Mossi's office. Mossi answered.

"Mossi here."

"Detective Mossi, this is Chance again and I think our suicide case may have taken a new turn."

"How so?"

"I'm not sure yet but it looks to me like Tom Dumar's cabin was right at the center of that fire in Laurel Canyon."

Chance could hear Mossi's chair squeak loudly...... probably moving to his computer screen. He heard keys being punched in a staggered hunt and peck style.

Mossi said, "You might be right about that."

Chance said, "Any injuries or fatalities yet?"

"Hold on a minute; I'll get an update."

Chance heard the line go into the blank infinity of hold, which allowed him to search his street signs more closely. Madison probably has one of those satellite guidance systems, he thought. I like the old-fashioned "seek and ye shall find" method. While still on hold he repeated the phrase to himself.

Seek and ye shall find.

Amazing how many everyday phrases originated in the Bible. He'd have to ask his sister Nikki more about that. And he still hadn't resolved the question he had about Gibbon's religion. Somehow he and Nik had moved away from that subject too quickly.

Mossi was back. "No fatalities, no injuries, not even any smoke inhalation cases. The Dumar cabin was empty but completely burned down."

"Do me a favor," said Chance. "Get someone out there right now to find what you can find."

"First of all that won't be much," said Mossi. "Even if this was arson, and they're looking hard at that already, there would have been a point to the arson, no?"

"If it's not insurance, the point would be to conveniently destroy things that might reopen the case of the Dumar suicide."

"Exactly. So the best time for a team to look would have been *before* the fire."

Chance sighed. Why was Mossi making this point when it was Mossi himself who failed to investigate the death? He pulled up a block away from Gibbon's house and parked on the opposite side of the street. He wanted to finish his talk with Mossi before even thinking about Gibbon.

"There still may be something we don't know," said Chance. "I'd especially like to know if Tom's office computer had been moved there. You could probably tell that."

"How do you know it wasn't in his office?"

"I went there to look. That's where I found your card. In the USC wastebasket."

"You USC people always think you're smarter than everybody else," said Mossi. "There's a reason John Wooden coached at UCLA. He wanted real people from the real world around him."

"How real is it to close a case and call it a suicide before you look into other options?"

Chance regretted the remark as soon as he said it. If he was going to find the truth quickly he wouldn't help open things up by sparring with Mossi. He tried a more conciliatory approach.

"You know what, Detective? I'm not against you here. I'm not even a USC guy; I'm University of Detroit. I told you that. Even more real world than UCLA. And I used to do what you do for a living, so I can sympathize. Cases back up. You want them closed so you can move on. But this was a client and a friend of mine, and he was definitely not ready to leave us. What if you and I were to help each other on this?"

Mossi said nothing.

Chance said, "Or not. Your call."

Mossi finally said, "See me tomorrow. After two. I have a case in Las Vegas but I'll be back."

"See you after two."

21

Chance sat quietly behind the wheel. One more call to Susan Dumar's phone and no answer. It went right to voice mail. At least she wasn't home during the fire. What a week this was turning out to be for Susan. He couldn't wait to see her and put his arm around her just to help her keep her sanity. Make her feel safe.

Despite all the misadventures he saw during his police days, Chance always thought that California was a pretty safe place to be. An amazingly huge percentage of people live here way past their seventies. Almost everybody, in fact. Right now living into your eighties was becoming the norm. Most people live long lives and then die in soft sheets and comfortable beds.

Not so for Tom.

And who knew who else would be brought down by whatever this misadventure was?

Evil has a way, thought Chance, of producing a whole chain of unintended consequences. He thought back to the O.J. Simpson case that occurred just before Chance was just entering the academy. One evil act and the ripple effect still hasn't stopped. One swift act of sexual rage designed to kill the angry beast in one man's chest instead unleashed a whole chain of bad events. Chance shook his head when he thought back on the jury that had been emotionally swept up by O.J.'s lawyers' attempt to make it a civil rights case.

The whole judicial system has become too politicized, he thought, but it will change. Chance needed to shake that thought off and return focus to himself.

The best possibility for change is always in the individual. Wu Li had taught him that. Wu Li had trained him in martial combat and said all strength was on the *inside*, as well as all enemies.

He snapped out of his thoughts when he saw the blue Taurus pull into the front drive at Gibbon's house. It was a fairly modest home for someone who had made so much money leveraging real estate deals. But the historical neighborhood was classy and cozy, with huge cottonwood trees giving shade to the street and front yards.

The man who got out of the car wasn't Gibbon, but looked a little like him. He was pudgy like Gibbon, and his puffed-out face was topped with bright red hair, the color of California carrots when they're ripe. This was the same guy Chance saw in the car that was tailing him two days ago.

Chance sat for another fifteen minutes before deciding not to go in. He had learned enough for the moment and wasn't sure how to make the most of going to the house right now. Would they both be there? Would he want to confront them together? Just for tailing him? Did he want to scare them off?

Maybe it would be better to just ease on down the road for now and remain under the radar. The sun had almost set completely and Chance thought about going past Gibbon's house slowly with his lights off until he got to the next block. Then he chuckled and thought that would look unusually stealthy to anyone peering out of a window. *It's been so long since I've done this*, he thought. A simple stakeout. You'd think one would have a kind of muscle memory.

Good sense finally kicked in.

He turned his lights on, backed his MG into a driveway made up of pea stones and listened to them crunch under his tires as he drove out in the other direction. He thought of his golden dog Angie and looked forward to relaxing at home and just letting life happen for a while.

After all, he wasn't a cop anymore.

That was the whole point of his life now.

He didn't really have to do anything about crime. He liked that status. Neutral. It was always the most creative place to come from.

22

Susan Dumar finally called Chance at five minutes after ten that night. He and Angie the dog were watching the evening news accounts of the fire in Laurel Canyon. Only five homes were lost completely, the most tragic, according to the newscasters, was a home that used to belong to Mama Cass. Chance knew that house was only fifty yards from the Dumar home.

"This is Susan and I'm sorry but my phone has been crazy, Robert; I just shut it down for a while."

"Are you okay?"

"Oh I'm fine. I was at my sister's in Santa Barbara when this happened. I drove out to the canyon, but they wouldn't let me in."

"Rusty?" Rusty was Tom and Susan's Irish setter.

"With me all the way, thank God," said Susan. "We had some fish in the cabin, but that's it."

"Fish! They're cajun now."

"No, boiled I bet, but we are doing the sick humor thing again, which you always seem to bring out......"

"Like learning the fees of the death coach."

"I should ask the death coach about dealing with the fish."

Chance could hear a kind of frantic relief in Susan's voice joking about this latest catastrophe in her life. He knew she was comfortable enough to keep talking to him, and he wanted to talk. He switched the TV to mute just as the fire chief was being interviewed and Angie looked up at him wondering if he knew the sound was off.

"Susan, what do you think happened here?"

"I think it was an accident," she said. "I know they're looking for arson; I saw the news...... but I can't imagine our house being involved. I can't imagine anything in that house worth getting rid of."

"What about you?"

"Do you think I'm worth getting rid of?"

"You're worth a lot, Susan. Especially if Tom's death is not what it looked like."

"You know, Robert, I thought a lot about that. I thought about his ungrammatical note, and as much as I'd love to believe he didn't take his own life, I've decided I just might not agree with you. You're basing it on one incorrect pronoun and..."

"No, no." Chance spoke slowly and carefully. "It's way more than that. I'm basing this on my work with Tom — my coaching sessions. They were vulnerable and deep. And he was gaining strength. He was not losing his will to live, Susan. Quite the opposite. He was getting really feisty. I almost had to hold him back."

"I know you're good Robert, and I know how bad you must feel coaching him and having him do this, but I just want some peace here. I just want to move on now."

"And so your house just accidentally burned down? In your mind it's just been a really bad week? You don't see anything strange in any of this?"

"I'm tired, Robert. I have to get the family together for the interment at the church. I have a lot to do. And I know that you want this to be different than it is. We all do."

"What *interment* are you talking about? Weren't you going to hold off on the cremation?"

"Too late, Robert. It's done. Life moves on."

Chance didn't like the feeling he was getting in his stomach. It was a feeling he hadn't had in a long time. It was a feeling that he used to rely on during interrogations of "persons of interest" because although it was uncomfortable, it always alerted him to the presence of a liar. That he was getting this feeling with Susan Dumar made him *very* uncomfortable, and he didn't totally trust himself on the phone with her right now so he looked for a quick exit.

"When's the church service?" he said.

"Next Saturday at 10 a.m. at Our Lady of Carmel. You know his church. I'm sending emails. You'll get one. There's also a place on the mortuary's website for you to put a remembrance of Tom. I'd love it if you did. It's Palm Sunday mortuary."

"Palm Sunday," said Chance. "I certainly will. And now you better get some rest."

"Thank you, Robert; you too."

Chance put the phone away and stared at the mute TV screen. A happy elderly couple was dancing in their kitchen as a pharmaceutical company's logo came on the screen. He was sorry he missed the voice over about the side effects, always his favorite part.

He clicked the TV off and Angie looked up at him to see if he knew what he had done. He scratched behind her ears and got up to walk into his office where he sat down at the computer screen. He went to the Palm Sunday mortuary website to see the page they had set up to record remembrances of Tom Dumar.

He wasn't about to enter anything right now.

Because if he did, and he was honest, he would say, "There's something wrong with all of this and we ought not rest until Tom's death and life receive a little more honor than you all are giving him with these premature sweet suicide condolences."

23

Glen Gibbon hated airports. People going through security were always so confused and flummoxed by such an easy process.

What's going on in their rattled minds? They're thinking: *What? My shoes, too? Take off my shoes?* Yes, everyone. Every time. Ever since Richard Reid tried to light his own shoe-bomb on fire in flight.

Gibbon hated terrorists, too. Idiots like Reid. Their stupidity. How technologically challenged they all were. They were cave men with civilization-envy. He wished he could be in charge of the drones that were killing terrorists now. He would love that remote-control extermination project.

He passed through the security archway and held his boarding pass up for the security guard to check. He hated how wimpy and symbolic security guards were.

Gibbon hated a lot of people, it turned out… almost everyone he encountered.

Except her.

The woman he was now counting on.

Gibbon found his way to his emergency exit seat in the coach section and put his carry-on in the overhead compartment. He liked being able to stretch his legs. And would he be willing to open that emergency exit door in case of trouble?

You bet he would.

He'd *love* being the first one out of the plane.

He wouldn't even mind jamming the door back in place after he exited so that all the human vermin who were following him would have to stay on board and deal with their deepest fears.

Gibbon only half-listened to the announcements being made. Then the captain came on to talk about the weather in Denver. Why was he called our captain? He was just a guy with a flying job. He was a pilot, that was true. But our captain? She actually said "your captain." Gibbon hated the human ego in all its forms.

He looked out the window at the orange-vested workers pulling the tiny service vehicles away from the plane. It started to hit him. *This is really happening.*

He cleared his throat and shook his head. He didn't want to jinx anything by over-fantasizing. One step at a time. He learned that at the evangelical boot camp in his church. One step at a time. Like Jacob's ladder. One step closer to heaven. His thoughts turned to his son. Home now, the Taurus and the house all his.

Would he be able to hold up?

Gibbon didn't exactly hate his son, but it took a lot of work not to. A lot of work. His own father used to tell him it would. "It will take a lot of work, Glen, not to hate your children. Even *more* work not to hate your wife."

Gibbon didn't still hate his wife because she blessed him with a divorce ten years ago and he never heard from her since. Too bad his son Gary looked so much like her, or he could have forgotten her forever. Gibbon hated it that Gary wasn't able to follow Robert Chance in a car without being found out.

Give him one simple thing to do.

But that guy Chance was demonic. Faking a broken-down engine in the middle of traffic. He had to have been faking that. Getting out of his car and walking down the line of cars behind him until he could look right into Gary's eyes. Gary ran, of course. And Chance got the license plate number.

Well, I won't have Chance to worry about any longer.

Gibbon looked at his boarding pass stub. "Brock Young" was the name on the pass. That would be his new identity in Denver. He picked the name out himself. And it amazed him all the forgeries and other dark services that were available to someone who knows how to use the internet.

Gibbon's heart stopped for a second.

Did he delete everything before he left? He should have burned the whole computer. His mind went back. He remembered his last hours at home and yes, he deleted everything.

He sat back and wondered if he could enjoy this flight that was carrying him into such a strange new future.

 **24**

Chance was, at that same moment, wondering and asking Madison Kerr about deleted computer files.

"Deleting isn't all that effective," said Madison as Chance pulled a chair over for her to sit in next to his couch. The golden dog Angie breathlessly wagged her tail until Madison gently pushed her into a seated position on the rug.

"She likes my clients," said Chance nodding at Angie. "My friends, she's neutral about. She knows where the dog food comes from."

Madison smiled at Angie and tickled behind her ears.

"Gibbon's final deletes involved two transactions with sites that make fake identification," she said. "He got a full ID kit for a 'Brock Young.'"

"Brock Young? It so doesn't fit him," said Chance.

"Well, I think he's Brock Young now," said Madison. "Besides, maybe that kind of name was the point. I don't think self-honesty would be a strong suit with a forger. You expected what kind of name, Killer Kowalski?"

"So when you delete, it doesn't fully eliminate information."

"No," said Madison. "You're catching on! Next we'll teach you to Google."

"I can't wait."

"If the fire was arson," said Madison, "and he was involved, I'm a little confused. Because if he has a thing for Susan Dumar you wouldn't think he'd burn her house down."

"Maybe he'd just huff and he'd puff," said Chance.

"I'm trying to be serious… trying to do serious investigative analysis."

"Free association doesn't hurt. We're seeking some big picture epiphanies. Linear thought always misses the holographic pattern."

Madison shook her head, got up, and walked to the window. She looked out at the trees. There were lemon and orange trees.

"Can you eat those oranges?"

"I don't know."

"You don't *know*? They're your trees." She stared at the whole yard. "They're beautiful."

"You know about trees and gardens?"

"I had a calamondin orange tree that I thought died, but I never got around to clearing it out."

"And what happened?"

"It weirdly came back to life."

Chance looked up and said nothing.

Madison continued, "There was this green stuff, shoots and sprigs and tiny sprouty things bursting out of the dead branch. New life where there had been total death."

"I wouldn't even know what a calamondin orange tree was, I don't think."

"Well, they're amazing. Calamondin oranges are healing agents in Chinese medicine. And they make the perfect marmalade."

"I'll trust that they do."

"So, Robert, how do you care for these beautiful trees if you know nothing about them?"

"My gardener comes. He cares for the living things and clears everything else away. I let him have whatever. Oranges. Lemons. Worms even, sometimes. He's a fisherman, he tells me. A *pescador*."

"It's amazing," Madison turned back from the window to look at Chance, who was beginning to tempt Angie with a rubber bone. "It's amazing to me how much you *don't* know. Willfully, I'm starting to think! You almost don't *want* to know. And yet with important things, like wisdom or insight, you're almost psychic."

"Sometimes that's just faster for me. Can I ask you something about what *you* know? Like computers?"

"Sure."

"Would a fire delete everything?"

"It would if it burned up the computer, of course. Are you thinking about Tom's computer that was missing from his office?"

"No I'm not. I don't believe that one will ever be found."

"Then what?"

"Susan's computer. That's the computer I would have liked to see."

"Tell me why."

Chance spent the rest of their time together explaining his gut reaction to Susan's whole demeanor around the death of her husband, and how quickly she had the cremation done when she said she wouldn't. He talked about Tom's suspicions a year ago... suspicions that he just remembered... that Susan was having an affair with a younger man.

Madison then went back through her files she'd copied from Gibbon's computer with photos of Susan. No emails from her that could be found. But she'd learned to trust Chance's intuitions.

 **25**

Detective Anton "Tony" Mossi agreed to meet Chance at the outdoor café of a Whole Foods market store on Wilshire in Santa Monica. The market took up a whole city block. They took a small table by a flower stand and the smell of pink roses mixed with that of the steaming coffee.

"We make mistakes," said Mossi, dipping his miniature tongue depressor into his paper cup of coffee. He took a bite from a blueberry bagel he had smeared with butter. "We move too quickly. We're pressured to close cases. It becomes like a business. Some guys just start punching time clocks."

"Instead of fighting crime and protecting the public," said Chance.

"You could put it that way."

"I've been there. So don't worry about it now."

"Why did you become a cop anyway? I mean, at the start."

"I wanted to protect the rights of people who were being abused. People who were being bullied. I wanted to stand up for them."

Mossi nodded.

"Bullied yourself when you were younger?" said Mossi.

"Big time."

Mossi looked at Chance's impressive upper body build and said.

"Not much any more."

"Never again, actually."

"How did you turn things around for yourself?"

"I found a guy. His name is Wu Li. Martial artist. Personal trainer. Chinese philosopher. At 145 pounds still the most lethal human weapon you'll ever meet. He took me under his wing. Broke me down and built me back up to where I could take care of myself."

Mossi nodded and smiled. He reached into his back pocket and pulled out a folded sheet of paper. He unfolded it and studied it for a moment.

"We picked up a suspect in the arson fire in the canyon," said Mossi. "He's waiting at the station right now."

"That's a good start," said Chance. "How did you find him?"

"Neighbor turned him in. Turns out his next-door neighbor was a real snoop and she saw him load some gas cans into his pickup that morning and then saw him come back that day with soot and ashes all over him looking 'like a chimney sweep,' she said. She said he looked like Dick Van Dyke in *Mary Poppins*."

"So he's a real pro."

"Right. But I have a question for you, Chance."

Chance noticed that Mossi was averting his eyes while squirming a little in his metal wicker chair. A group of teenage girls walked by and caught Mossi's attention. There were four of them and it sounded like each one of them was yelling the words, "No way!" to the other three.

No way, thought Chance.

But there may *be* a way I can work with this guy Mossi. He seems to be trying to make an apology today.

"Anyway," said Mossi, his focus back on Chance. "I checked up on you a little bit more after you left the other day, and I got a lot of mixed reviews."

"Understandable," said Chance. "I'm never very consistent."

"No, some guys swore by you, said you were the best investigator they ever worked with."

"And the others?"

"Well…" Mossi was looking for the right words. "They said you were old-school, hard line. 'Captain America,' one called you. You wouldn't cut any slack. You wouldn't let them just be cops."

"I can see that," said Chance. "Given some people's loose definition of being a cop. Anyway, what is it you wanted to ask me?"

"Will you help me interrogate this guy? I mean, I don't need help. Believe me. But if your reputation is that you're the best interrogator who ever lived…"

"What's special about this guy? What could be all that intimidating about Dick Van Dyke?"

Mossi shifted again and drained his coffee. He wasn't practiced at asking for help.

"It's not just him," he said. "It's me these days. I'm good but lately I don't do well with most of the people I go into the box with. There's something about me that seems to shut people right up."

"You think?" said Chance, remembering Mossi's aggressive and obnoxious mocking of the coaching profession in their first meeting. Chance had told him he wasn't a very happy person, and Chance meant it. One doesn't judge, mock, scorn and become verbally aggressive without having a lot of unhappiness that needs to be downloaded.

Chance suddenly wished this case didn't exist. He wished it was over. It had exploded into complexity – almost like the crude amateur bombs built with tacks and shattered marbles in them, meant to cause maximum pain to innocent people.

Every crime had a ripple effect like this one.

There was always collateral damage.

Usually criminals miss that part when they're making their plans. Then after they're forced to get clean and sober in prison they have time to see, in retrospect, all the damage. The burden of the guilt is so great they don't know what to do with it. When they do get released… and judges these days just love to release them... they drink alcohol and use drugs again just to quiet the demons of guilt, and the whole cycle repeats itself with more collateral damage.

Put the *judge* in jail next time and see what happens.

That would be Chance's first step in cleaning up the judicial system.

"I'm clumsy," said Mossi, in an awkward way, unintentionally proving his point.

"One of the reasons I love the coaching work I now do," said Chance, "is that it's still a form of interrogation. It's a positive version of what I used to do. I ask questions, but now I do it to find someone's hidden strength, not to break criminals. Questions get people to truth and reality faster than anything I've ever seen."

"But do people want that?"

"Not always," said Chance. "Not at the start."

Chance gave Mossi a long look and smiled. When people said the word "people," as in *do people want that*, they usually mean themselves. Mossi was as transparent to Chance as a little child, and that made his heart go out to him. Like the comic sadness of a little boy trying to lie his way out of trouble, Mossi looked temporarily vulnerable behind his tough-cop exterior. Chance caught himself thinking he would love to take him on as a client. Chance wanted this case to be over so he could go back to helping people.

"I mean," said Mossi, "it seems like people would be afraid of getting to reality too quickly."

"They are," said Chance. "But it's just the idea they hold of it. That's what they're afraid of, their own idea. Reality becomes like the monster under the bed, for most people. They have made up scary stories about it. When they really face it they are amazed."

"At what?"

"They realize that reality is on their side. Reality is supportive. Like water. Like when you learn how to swim.

Your body learns that the water is there for you, for support. Life is like that, too, in reality."

"Well, it sounds too good to believe. But I will give you one thing, you made a name for yourself as an interrogator, so, again, I am here today to ask a favor."

"Anything."

"Will you interrogate our arsonist with me? I want to experience what it is that you do because I'm pretty impatient. And the transcripts I found of some of your interrogations were fairly bizarre. You have to admit, you don't do it by the book."

"I guess I just go wherever the suspect takes me. The right questions can create a clearing for the bad guy to dance in, and some of them have never really danced since they were kids."

"See, there you are. You lost me completely with that. You make it sound like some Zen thing where nothing means anything."

"Nothing is what I'm after," said Chance.

Mossi rolled his eyes in mock disgust. He slowly shook his head. He looked out at the street. All the cars had slowed to a stop for a pedestrian in the crosswalk. He shook his head again. He said, "California. In New York you floor it when there's too much riff raff in the street and watch them scatter. You teach them a lesson. The street is for cars. Cross at the light or watch out."

"I like California," said Chance.

"Ride over with me?"

"To headquarters? How about I'll meet you there. What floor will we be on? I'm not familiar with the new building."

"Headquarters is on Main, but enter at Second and Spring, and just meet me in the lobby. I'll take you up."

The cop and the ex-cop got up to shake hands. Mossi smiled and gripped Chance's hand for an extra second. Reality was feeling good today.

26

Chance and Detective Mossi stood outside the interrogation room looking at the arson suspect, Rico Hornsby, on the video monitor outside the room. He obviously didn't know he was being observed. Hornsby had his head down on the table and kept opening and closing his hands as if the handcuffs were burning his wrists.

"What was the final word from the fire investigators?" Chance said.

Mossi said, "Definitely perpetrated. Definitely deliberately set, might have been started in the eucalyptus outside the Dumar cabin. But lots of help within. Lots of accelerant."

"That big tree was all over the house. It held the house in the palm of its hand. What do you have on this guy besides his neighbor's observations?" said Chance.

A uniformed officer seated at a computer next to the video monitor that showed Hornsby (now lifting his head and breathing deeply) pulled two sheets from her printer and handed one each to Chance and Mossi.

"Four priors," she said. "Nothing too heavy. Shoplifting. Public nuisance. Etc."

"What's his story for the time line?" said Chance.

Mossi laughed, "He was *trying to help*. He says he sensed some trouble in the canyon and drove in to see if he could help."

"Did he have his cell phone with him? Because we can track his calls and the towers he was closest to for each of the calls to check the validity of his story about his movements."

"My younger guy is already on that," said Mossi. "Those kids of things are uncharted waters for me."

"As long as you've got someone who will do it. You don't want to be so old school you let people slip away. Wouldn't be fair to the public you are sworn to protect."

"I get that," said Mossi.

"Good, let's go in and talk to him."

"First this," said Mossi, handing Chance a document. "Sign this form. It puts you on the case as an expert witness and special consultant to my department so the interviews won't be tossed."

Chance signed his name and both men walked around to the hall entrance to the room. A uniformed officer nodded at Mossi and punched a code into the box by the door and both men entered.

"Rico Hornsby?" said Mossi, extending his hand to the young man who looked more frightened than anyone Chance could remember. He had wild long hair and one of those grunge band beards that you never knew how intentional it was. Forgot to shave for a week? Or are you Kurt Cobain?

"Richard," said Hornsby. "It's Richard. People say Rico but I don't like that."

"Richard," said Mossi, taking a chair on the opposite side of the prisoner. He motioned at Chance to take the chair next to him, "Richard this is Robert Chance, a consultant to the department for this case. He's going to have a few questions for you."

Hornsby looked at Chance. He said, "Like a psychic? I saw that once on TV; a detective brought in a psychic to solve a case."

"Like a psychic, yes," Mossi smiled, looking over at Chance.

Chance said, "I'm simply a consultant who works on these type of cases, Richard."

Honsby nodded.

Chance studied Richard Hornsby's eyes and body language and noticed that he was still twisting his wrists inside the cuffs on his hands. He asked him, "Can I remove those cuffs for you, Richard? They don't look very comfortable. That okay with you, Detective Mossi?"

"Sure," said Mossi, who stepped outside the door and then came back with a key and took the cuffs off of Hornsby. Hornsby rubbed his wrists and nodded to Chance. He was grateful.

To Chance, an initial bonding gesture like this was always a good way to begin an interview. Chance said to Hornsby, "Where were you when this fire started, Richard?"

"I was at home with my girlfriend Monica, and we were getting her ready to go to LAX to fly out to see her mother."

Chance let a few beats pass until Mossi twisted in his chair to look at him. This was it? You just take your time?

Chance said, "Richard, how did you know what you just told me?"

"What do you mean?"

"You told me what you were doing when the fire started. How did you know when the fire started?"

"Oh, oh, yeah, I see what you mean. Well I *didn't* know. I didn't have any idea, but, you know."

"You guessed."

"Right. I guessed because on my way back from the airport I saw the smoke and that's when I went to see if I could help."

"You didn't go home first?"

"No. Well, wait. Now I don't remember."

"You were seen putting gas containers in your truck at your home earlier in the day."

"Right. In case I run out. I do that."

Chance nodded to Richard like it all made perfect sense.

"What did you think of the fire?" Chance was reaching in his folder for a yellow pad and pulling a pen from his pocket.

"What did I think of it?"

"Yes."

"I don't know what you mean. It was big. It was a bad thing. And I just wanted to help."

"If I told you about who died in that fire, what would you think?"

"That didn't happen! I know that didn't happen."

"Just answer my question. If you learned later that someone died because of that fire, what would you think of it?"

"I'd be bummed!"

"What do you believe should be the punishment for someone who started a fire that killed someone? Let's say Monica was killed in a fire that someone started. What should the punishment be?"

Chance knew from experience that when he was talking to the guilty party, this kind of question always resulted in a very minimal expression of punishment.

Hornsby said, "Well, you'd have to be sure they really started it, and even if they did, if they never meant no harm to no one, I don't think punishment should be that big. For an accident. Just my opinion."

"What made you go into the canyon to help?"

"I saw the smoke."

"You saw it or you smelled it? Because if I know my LA, your drive back from the airport would not ..."

"I smelled it."

Chance made notes. He took his time. He looked back up at Richard.

"How are you doing right now financially, Richard? Do you have a job?"

"Odd jobs."

"And your wife?"

"Girlfriend. Monica works at Motor Vehicle. We don't have much."

"And you've been in a little trouble, I see."

"In my drinking days, yes."

"You're sober now?"

"One hundred and twelve days, yes, sir."

"Rigorous self-honesty?"

"Yes. And I've heard that said in meetings. Are you a friend of Bill's?"

"Very close friend," said Chance.

Chance knew that people recovering from alcohol addiction often use the code "Are you a friend of Bill W?" to see if the person they are talking to is in the same program without breaking their anonymity. Chance was not in the program, but a coaching client had once been. He had learned a lot in his two Al-Anon support group meetings, so much so that he now considered Bill a friend.

Chance put his pen down and turned his chair toward Mossi. He turned back to Richard Hornsby and shook his head.

"Did your father drink?" Chance said. Mossi stared at him with a blank look.

Richard didn't know how to answer. Finally he said, "My father drank all the time."

"Still alive?"

"No."

"Died drunk?"

"Yes."

"And you?"

"What?"

"Will you die drunk?"

"I don't know what you mean. I just told you, I have 112 days. I have a good program. If you're in the program too you know what I mean…"

"Because you *will* die drunk, Richard. You know that."

Rico Hornsby stared down at the table. Then back up at Chance.

Chance raised his voice a few degrees, "You know what I'm talking about Richard, don't you? You can lie to *us* all day long but if you can't be honest with yourself you will drink again won't you? And you will die drunk and it will be worse than you can know."

Richard said nothing.

Chance said, "How often do you run out of gas?"

"What?"

"That you need to put gas containers in your pick-up. How often do you run out of gas?"

"Not that often."

"We have your truck, Richard. This is going to get real scary for you if you keep lying to Detective Mossi and me. You have to know who your friends are if you're going to survive this thing at all. You want to throw those 112 days away and start all over?"

Richard Hornsby rubbed his eyes but the tears came anyway. He couldn't stop thinking about his father, how his father had begged Richard to bring him vodka into the Veteran's hospital. What he smelled like. The lies he told.

The nightmare.

How did this psychic know all this? Psychics just do. He always thought the truth about being an alcoholic would have stopped his father from drinking, but it didn't.

Chance reached across the table, and put his hand on Richard's forearm. "If I were really hurting for money I would listen to just about anybody who offered me some," said Chance. "Especially if I was trying to stay sober, get out of debt. Make my life right. And especially if I could make sure that nobody was hurt."

"Nobody was hurt," said Richard.

"That's not true, Richard. That's no longer true."

The tears started to come again, which was maddening to Richard who no longer knew who to be.

Mossi spoke: "Richard, if someone convinced you to do this why don't you let me and Mr. Chance spend our time interrogating *them* instead of you. If you were paid to do this, or convinced some other way, we want to leave you alone so we can go bring *them* in. Not that you aren't responsible for your part. But let us do our real job."

Chance leaned back and relaxed. He was happy with where Mossi was going.

Richard looked at Chance. He said, "Nobody was hurt."

"Not true, Richard," said Chance. "I only wish that was true."

Richard covered his face with his hands.

Chance continued. "And I have spoken to the family. To a person who lost some loved ones. Have you ever lost loved ones, Richard?"

Mossi started to speak but Chance held his hand up slightly and shook his head. Hornsby's head was down on the table. Silence was all that was needed now. And Chance was willing to wait for as long as it took, because the more silence there was the heavier it got in the room.

"No, I never have," said Hornsby. "Lost a loved one in a fire."

"Who had you do this?" said Chance.

"Gibbon," Hornsby said.

"Glen Gibbon?" said Chance.

"*Gary* Gibbon. Gary Gibbon gave me a thousand dollars up front and owes me a thousand more."

 **27**

Mossi and Chance sat in the station conference room on the floor above the interrogation units. Mossi was drinking a can of peach-flavored iced tea and Chance drank deeply from a plastic bottle of water.

"Lost in the fire?" said Mossi. "I mean, it's technically true that we don't have to tell a suspect the truth, but where did you get that?"

"It *was* the truth," said Chance. "They were fish, but they died… in their tank in Susan Dumar's house. And who are we, in our arrogance, to elevate human lives above the lives of fish?"

"That Rico Hornsby is going to be some kind of pissed when he learns from his jail buddies what you were referring to."

"Enhanced interrogation," said Chance

"Is that what it is?" said Mossi. "Because I couldn't even follow what you were doing. What was that stuff about his father dying a drunk? How did you know that? And why would he relate that to this, anyway? I thought you were off the beaten track a few times in there. How can I learn when I don't get what you do?"

"The beaten track is what they have already rehearsed answers for. You don't want rehearsed answers. You want to break the paradigm as often as you can without losing your bond. In fact, you can do it while increasing the bond. The bond itself, in the end, is what's going to open him up."

Mossi began laughing and shaking his head.

"Okay. Thanks for nothing. Remind me not to have you teach a class in this. I get that I've got a lot to learn, but it doesn't look very teachable."

"It is. Just let yourself understand it on a deeper level than logic if you can."

Mossi picked up a piece of yellow paper and gestured with it. "Thanks for this Gary Gibbon's address. I have patrol on it right now; we'll bring him in. You want to be here when we talk to him?"

"Yes, but I may not ask him anything."

"You may not? Why not?"

"I want to watch you do it."

 28

Madison Kerr was dressed in a pale blue business suit as she stood up in front of the boardroom of Geneticore, her biggest and best client. She had just finished another consulting session in which she taught them their final steps in converting from brochures, print and broadcast media over to Facebook, Twitter, MySpace, targeted blogs, and various other internet networking systems.

"Won't these fads fade out?" said the silver-haired CEO Bernie Sanborn.

"Yes, of course they will," said Madison. "And that's the exciting part. Staying ahead of what's next, instead of fighting it, or regretting it. Dropping what fades out, riding what fades in. MySpace may be gone as we speak. But our competitors will move more slowly than we do if we do this right. For the past two years we've been fighting it and our sales show the result."

Madison had decided long ago to always address her clients as "we" instead of "you." She wanted them to appreciate that she was part of the team the minute they paid her retainer, and the inclusive language made her more responsible for results and outcomes.

As the meeting came to a finish three of the executive committee members came to the front of the room to shake her hand. She thanked them as she was shutting down her PowerPoint and laptop. They said they'd never seen her this forceful and well prepared.

Somehow it didn't thrill her or even surprise her to hear that.

She opened her cell phone as soon as everyone left the room. There was a text from Chance.

"Koi pond 7 p.m?"

She texted back immediately. "You'd be proud. I'm making $. Abundance no longer needed. C/U @7."

 **29**

The metal tables by the koi pond at the Fairmont Miramar were chilly and moist with dew from the ocean. Chance and Madison were glad to be finished with their wait in the lobby. They were there for ten minutes before getting a table. It seemed like there was some kind of convention in town and the hotel was buzzing with people wearing name tags and Hawaiian shirts.

"I love themes," said Madison as they sat down in the middle of tables filled with Hawaiian-shirted outdoor drinkers and diners.

"You do?"

"Yes, it's like grade school all over. This is American Revolution Week and we all dress like Martha Washington for a day."

"Even the boys?"

"The boys were George. And Ben Franklin."

"What do you suppose this convention is about?"

Madison stretched in her chair to see if she could read a name tag.

"Insurance underwriters something and something," she said.

"Sounds like almost too much fun. Hawaii is such an original theme. Maybe they'll all get a DVD of *Blue Hawaii*."

"Oh, I love that movie," said Madison. "It was my grandma's favorite. She'd watch it with me when I was little. Angela Lansbury plays Elvis's mom. It's so innocent. Elvis sings, what was it, oh yes, 'Moonlight Swim.' Do you think America was ever really like that? That's back from an era I can't even conceive of. Elvis inviting you to go on a moonlight swim."

Chance tried not to picture that swim. Then he noticed for the first time that Madison's eyes weren't actually totally blue. Not completely. There were little flecks of gold he had never seen before. Imagine that. Do the flecks only come out at night?

"Earth to Robert," she said. "Do you think America was ever really like that?"

"Like what?"

"Like *Blue Hawaii.*"

"It's whatever you want it to be. This country. You create America when you wake up. America is you and me right now."

"Okay, whatever. But don't you think these conventions are kind of silly, given the times we're living in?"

"They seem okay to me. Just the right thing for these people. It gives them a break. Can you imagine writing insurance...?"

Chance stopped in the middle of his sentence and reached under the table for his yellow pad and put it between the water glass and the silverware. On top of a fresh page he wrote the word: *insurance.*

Madison craned her neck to read the word. She leaned back in her chair.

"Insurance?" she said. "Do you think the arson was about insurance? I thought we were thinking more along the lines of trying to get rid of evidence, or something."

Chance nodded his head. He said, "Yes, we are. But to stay fresh, let's pretend this whole thing has been about collecting money from somewhere."

"That just never ceases to amaze me," said Madison. "That people would burn things down or kill other people just for money."

"That shouldn't amaze you, really," said Chance. "Look at your own version of it."

Madison tilted her head quickly. It reminded Chance of one of the things he liked best about Angie his golden retriever... how she would tilt her head just a little whenever she was questioning anything.

"My own version of *what*? Burning cabins in Laurel Canyon and killing people?"

"Your own version of irrational money behavior."

"Am I to feel guilty about that now?"

"No, no. You are to enter the mind of the suspect like a great investigator would, relating their brain to yours and seeking to recognize patterns. Just relate and explore."

"Okay. That's better. But speaking of what is and isn't related, I've got to tell you something. Ever since I took your retainer for investigating this Gibbon case, the other part of my business has immediately improved. Picked up considerably."

"I thought it would," said Chance. "And I'm really glad it did."

"You *thought* my business would pick up? Even before I told you it had? So you just know *everything* in advance? Why do I bother living it out? I can just ask you what's going to happen."

"I'm sensing some hostility."

"How… or why… did you know my other business, my internet consulting, would get better?"

"Because of what we've been talking about," said Chance, as he waved the approaching waitress away while giving her a "two more minutes" sign with his fingers. "People all have the same fear," he said. "Fear I won't make it. Fear I won't survive in a grown-up world. And that very fear pushes business away. Business is not attracted to fear. But when you got the investigation project, you relaxed your anxiety about the other business. And a relaxed person is a confident person and that is going to produce business."

"Well, you're right!" Madison noticed that she was nearly shouting. Two elderly Hawaiians turned to look at her. She took a breath and moved her chair closer to the table.

"You're right," she said more softly. "When I finished my last presentation to Geneticore, the CEO asked if I would consider going to London to work with his office there for two days."

"And you said?"

"And I said I didn't think I'd be able to right now and he called me the next day to find out when I *could* go and I decided to put him off, tell him no, by quoting a very large prepaid project fee."

"That's good. Like we've talked about, limitation creates value. People, especially men, want what they can't have."

"Then he said… I mean, I couldn't even believe I was hearing him say this, but he said he'd cut the check *that day* if I'd open my calendar…"

"And I hope you opened your calendar."

"Oh, it was already open."

"When are you going to London?"

"In exactly thirty days! Are you okay… are we okay with that? I'll be there two days."

"Yes!"

Now the waitress was at their table to take their orders. Chance ordered the deluxe ground beef burger, no bun, with cottage cheese and peas on the side and Madison ordered the seafood salad. Chance asked for coffee with real cream and Madison refreshed her mint tea. Chance looked at the conventioneers at a nearby table. They were getting louder by the minute.

"Why does alcohol make people louder?" he asked. "With each drink the volume increases."

Madison smiled. "They're deluded by a drug into thinking they are finally being listened to. Their voices get louder because the drug excites them. They are finally worth listening to. The next day they realize it was all delusion." She watched Chance move his yellow pad to the side of the table. She looked again at the word *insurance* he had so carefully printed at the top.

"So who held the insurance on the cabin?" she said. "Probably Tom and Susan?"

"Yes, I would guess."

"But arson, such an obvious arson, kind of rules insurance out, doesn't it? I mean, these are intelligent people. Insurance companies sometimes take years to agree to pay on a case of arson. If even then. As long as it's an open case, right? They would never collect anything. And didn't Tom already have a life insurance policy? Or does suicide nullify it?"

"Suicide would only nullify a recently obtained policy. I think in California it's usually two years. If you've had it for two years you can kill yourself."

"How pleasant. I just pictured a shattered piggy bank."

"How do you mean?"

"A piggy bank throwing itself off a tall dresser so it could break on the floor and spill its money out for someone else."

"You mean Tom might have killed himself for Susan's financial benefit? Thrown himself off the dresser so all the pennies would be hers? Worth a thought I guess. We can check all the insurance Tom and Susan had. Just for fun."

"How can you check things like that now that you're no longer a cop?"

"Oh, but I am! My new friend Detective Mossi gave me consultant status to this case. I can now check anything."

"Okay, fill me in. Tell me what you did at headquarters with Mossi, because when you first met with him I thought you said he was a total jerk. And bring me completely up to date, because I've got some new ideas of my own."

The Hawaiian shirts began to thin out and leave the koi pond. The noise level toned down, and the running of the pond water over the rocks started to make a nice backdrop to the flow of conversation as Chance filled Madison in on his interaction with Mossi and the suspect Richard Hornsby.

When they were finished they agreed to cancel their coaching session scheduled for eight the next morning and to use that time to go over Madison's ideas.

To Madison, no time in her life had ever passed this quickly.

30

Glen Gibbon closed his eyes the minute the flight attendant announced that they were making their descent into Denver. He hated flight attendants. They were never there when you really needed them; and when they *were* there, their smiles never seemed real. Whatever happened to the good old days when they were called stewardesses, a term meant only for a woman, and when they waited on me hand and foot like geishas, and always anticipated my every need.

Gibbon didn't know if any woman in the world had *ever* been real. In his experience they all wanted something. He pressed his temples with the palms of his hands trying to make his headache go away.

Was it the altitude or the hatred?

This pain always seemed to hit him when other people were being their most annoying.

The plane dropped out of the sky, or so it felt to Gibbon. Just a straight drop down. Breathtaking in the worst sense. Gibbon opened his eyes to see if the other passengers were as scared as he was. A plane falls out of the sky and these people are just chatting and laughing like nothing happened? Are they just morons? Morons oblivious to the danger. Lemmings going over a cliff. Pigs to slaughter. A well-deserved slaughter. Why wouldn't they have any sense of how vulnerable they are up here sitting like idiots in this huge 900,000-pound aluminum flying tube?

Gibbon hated clueless people.

He pulled an index card from his upper pocket where he had written down some words from the Talmud. Not exactly his religion, but he felt his life had broken out beyond his religion now. He had found these words while searching around the internet for ways to change his identity: "If a man feels that his evil passion is gaining mastery over him, let him go to a place where he is unknown."

Denver would make him unknown. Denver might even make it all better. Just like his mother used to say. She would always say she would "make it all better" until Gibbon got a little older and found out she couldn't any more. Maybe she never even meant that.

But Denver would not let him down like people do.

Because Denver was where he would be Brock Young.

No more Glen Gibbon, victim of other people's stupidity.

Brock Young would be in control. Like those guys who control the drones, the unmanned planes that kill terrorists in the Arab streets. Brock Young would control everything.

The man next to Gibbon must have weighed three hundred pounds. Gibbon tried not to look at him. But he couldn't help it. He was drawn to him. Drawn to his hatred of him. Why was he allowed to fly? Anything for a buck, these airlines don't care how uncomfortable they make others. He rubbed his temples again as he thought he heard the man speak. Southern accent, it sounded like. *Was he actually speaking to me? Even though my eyes were closed and I was rubbing my temples in obvious pain?*

The plane dropped again, and this time it felt like it dropped on top of something solid. Was that possible? Another plane? Gibbon looked out the window. He hated looking out the window, but he just had to see whether they had hit something. He saw dark clouds and a flash of lightning. *That can't be good.* What if he never made it to Denver? What if "Brock Young" were to perish in the sky? Who would they notify?

Gibbon started to chuckle at that thought.

Until he realized that the man next to him was speaking.

"So…is Denver home to you?"

Gibbon turned his head slowly toward the sound of the voice. His neck was aching. It was hard to turn it. Was it ever this hard to turn his head before? He finally got turned around enough to see a cheerful, heavy, very old man in a blue shirt and an olive drab cardigan sweater. The elderly aren't usually this heavy, thought Gibbon. Heavy people don't last that long. Too big a strain on the cardiopulmonary system, or so his ex-wife used to tell him every time he gained weight.

Is Denver home to me? Not to me. It's home to Brock Young, but why does this guy care?

Gibbon forced a smile.

"No, I'm just here for a little business," Gibbon said.

"Business or pleasure?"

Gibbon couldn't believe the man's question. Didn't he hear what he just said? *Hey guy, I just said I was here for business. Can't you refer to my previous answer, or do I really honestly have to talk to you again?*

Gibbon felt an unexpected tiny bolt of fear cross his chest. He pictured a future courtroom where this big man's testimony was being shown to a jury on videotape. "That picture? That's him. I flew right next to him all the way to Denver. Couldn't answer even the simplest questions."

Gibbon said, "I am here on business just like I said. Not pleasure this time. Because this time I'm here on business."

"What kind of business are you in?"

This had gone too far. Gibbon wanted a graceful exit but he couldn't get the courtroom out of his mind now. Now the big man was actually on the witness stand and the district attorney was questioning him, "So. When you asked the defendant what kind of business he was in, what did he say?"

Gibbon's mind was racing. He wanted to be invisible. He needed to be in control but he wasn't. That's because he wasn't Brock Young yet. He cleared his throat.

"I design planes, airplanes, unmanned aircraft, the drones. The ones you read about in Afghanistan."

"Goodness me. And of course you're in Pakistan, too."

"Pardon me?"

"I mean, you are a blessing! I heard Al-Qaeda was so spooked by your drones that they're doing all these new suicide bombings in Pakistan to try to get you to quit. Sir, I am honored to know you."

"You don't know me," said Gibbon, regretting immediately the tone with which he said it. Instead of being bland and forgettable he was being the opposite. He was losing control. Making a scene. He was classic Glen Gibbon.

Would Brock Young have done this?

Never.

Brock Young would have closed his eyes, muttered an apology and turned his back on the big guy so as never to be identified in the future.

But Glen Gibbon was typically out of control. Turning a small mess into a bigger one. Happened every time. Gibbon hated human communication. It was all so phony anyway. Then you had to appear real or authentic or at least friendly so people would move on. In Gibbon's mind, that was now the whole purpose of human communication. To get people to move on. To get them to leave you alone. Gibbon hated how this man's eyes were shining. *Oh my God he is extending his hand to shake mine.* Could this get any worse?

"Leonard Whitt," said the passenger next to Gibbon. "I am proud to know you."

"Brock Young," said Gibbon, shaking the largest hand he had ever shaken.

"I'm in law enforcement," said Leonard Whitt, not noticing that some of the color was beginning to leave Brock Young's face.

"Good deal," said Gibbon. "Now, if you'll excuse me."

He smiled a thin, strained smile at Leonard Whitt and reached for a small notebook in his briefcase, as if he had important work to do in the few minutes they had before landing.

"Retired," said Leonard. "I know what you were thinking."

He knew what I was thinking? Oh, tell me this feeling I have is just nerves and turbulence.

Leonard Whitt smiled and said, "I bet you were thinking that a man my size couldn't be in any respectable law enforcement organization you had heard of."

Gibbon forced another smile. He shrugged his shoulders like he was at a loss for words.

"Retired ten years ago," said Leonard. "Been feedin' myself ever since. Doctors say I'm diggin' my grave with a knife and fork."

Gibbon shook his head as if to say that life was very hard to make sense of. This time he was successful at twisting fully toward the window. Leonard Whitt sighed and opened his copy of *ESPN: The Magazine.*

Gibbon was glad this one particular nightmare had come to an end. If only he had been Brock Young with this guy from the start. But he'd learn. He'd learn to do life right. He'd learn to be in control.

 **31**

As Gibbon looked through the parting dark clouds to see the first signs of Denver his thoughts drifted to his redheaded son. He wondered about whether it was pragmatic or sinful to leave Gary in L.A. to deal with such a confusing conflagration there.

It would be confusing to Gary when they arrested him, which Gibbon knew they would.

But he would never have to see that red hair again reminding him *every time* of his ex-wife. The one who didn't turn out to be real. The redheaded woman who always told Gibbon he didn't sacrifice himself enough for her.

You want sacrifice, little lady? Read the story of Isaac. God asks Abraham to sacrifice his son.

Abraham agrees.

Starts to kill his own son!

Most painful moment in the whole Bible.

Then God laughs like Jim Carrey and says I WAS JUST MESSIN WITH YA!

Well, this sacrifice would be the real thing. He would sacrifice Gary. But that was not evil. Why? Because he was sacrificing himself, too. Glen Gibbon would be destroyed the minute this plane touched down and he walked through the jetway as Brock Young.

The plane dipped again in its final descent and then seemed to twist to the side and flip back as Gibbon grabbed his armrests.

Leonard Whitt was laughing. Gibbon looked at him.

The big retired law officer said, "Think we're going to make it?"

"God willing," mumbled Gibbon as he turned away from his imagined accuser.

32

Chance called his sister Nikki as soon as his meeting with Madison at the Fairmont Hotel was finished and he was sailing down the street in his open MG with the Pacific Ocean winds making him feel grateful for having been born.

"How early do you rise, Nik," he said, "I mean, what time in the morning do you have to leave for the shelter?"

"I'm up at 5:30 for morning meditation and all that, but I'm happy to see you any time."

"If I came by at six tomorrow, would that mess with your morning meditation? I have a client, or a meeting anyway, at eight but I'd like to finish our conversation."

"Six would be great. I'll have coffee on."

"Your meditation?"

"How about you just leave that to me?"

Chance laughed. As peaceful as Nikki was she was also the sturdiest person he had ever known. He was looking forward to meeting with her because he kept thinking there was something in Glen Gibbon's religious practices or poses that would help him find some answers. Nik knows all about that kind of thing.

33

"You would be wrong about that," said Nikki as she cleared the little poetry magazines off of her coffee table so she and her brother could put their drinks down. Chance sprawled on her couch and Nikki sat on a cushion on the floor on the other side of the blond wooden table.

"Wrong in what way?" said Chance with a twinkle beginning to enter his eyes. He loved being wrong. It always led to rapid learning. Being right lulled him to sleep and soon he was missing everything.

"Wrong about his religion having anything to do with anything," Nikki said. "If he makes a big deal out of being religious but doesn't follow the golden rule or any of the principles, you're just back to square one. Because it doesn't mean anything."

"I thought it might mean that people in his religious group are repressed, or overly manipulated and that it can cause people to rebel against all that forced good by being evil."

"Nice try."

"Not applicable?"

"Not at all. Even in my seminary with all of us studying to be in the ministry, everyone was different. The faith itself had nothing to do with it. His religion is actually quite beautiful."

"You've looked into it?"

"Yes, since we last met. And it is quite beautiful."

"Well, that just takes the air out of my balloon."

"You need an open mind, Robert, to be good at what you do. You've told me that yourself."

"It's just that whole religious question has been so hard for me to figure out."

"Don't figure it out. That's not where it is."

"Where is it?"

"It's an experience. True spirituality is an experience. You experience it or you don't. If you want to understand it, be open to experiencing it and stop trying to figure it out."

"Sounds a lot like falling in love."

"It's exactly like falling in love with one difference."

"What that?"

"It lasts."

34

Madison arrived at Chance's home office fifteen minutes early. She sat in her Volvo looking in the mirror in the visor and then flipped it back up. Why are you so worried about your new makeup? This isn't a date. This doesn't need to be like high school.

She took a deep breath and reached across to the passenger seat for her folder. The upper tab was labeled, "Monkey." She thought that was a kind of funny code for Gibbon and that Chance would probably laugh if he saw it. But she also thought it was smart, in case someone else glanced at her folder, someone who didn't need to know what she was working on.

She leafed through the information on the flammable eucalyptus trees, the cryptic exchanges with a "Garon" aka Gary on "The book of Revelations and the everlasting lake of torture" which she took to be an arrangement for the hell fire of arson.

She thought back to her agency days three years ago when Gibbon's real estate company was a client. She wasn't the primary account manager on his account, but because she was then a media buyer she sat in on a number of meetings in which Gibbon kept maniacally trying to get unheard-of discounts from various media buys. If the creative department or the production team made one mistake with one ad, no matter how small, no matter if the consumer couldn't possibly have noticed it, Gibbon always demanded a full refund. He would always threaten to take his business to another agency and finally

Madison's agency CEO let him. Madison wondered why they had waited so long.

Must be money fear, she thought. Who am I to judge it if I myself have it? When did my own money fear start? Why was it leaving me so fast?

She looked up and down Chance's street to see if she could see any bag ladies. Ever since she was a little girl and saw her first bag lady, she was terrified that some day she might be one.

She heard a tapping on her window that startled her so much she dropped her folder and all the papers scattered on the car floor. She looked up and saw Chance smiling and trying not to laugh. She rolled the window down. He stepped back with his hands out in mock surrender.

"Sorry!" he said. "I didn't mean to scare you. I saw your car and I thought you might want to start early."

"Of course," she said. "Give me a minute. I'll be right in."

Did she really want to do the whole mirror thing again? She watched Chance walk inside. She loved men in jeans, especially jeans and a white dress shirt with the sleeves rolled up. She shook herself awake. No mirror. Forget the jeans and shirt. Time to grow up, girl, and do some real work.

Chance had left the front door open with just the screen door to knock on. Before she could knock he yelled from inside for her to come in. Madison walked into the kitchen where he was making coffee and tea.

"Can you coach me on something before we start the criminal work?" she said.

"Of course."

"Where do you think someone's fear of being a bag lady would come from? It's almost embarrassing that it was such a real fear."

"Tell me what the fear is like," he said. "When you think about being a bag lady, what are you thinking? Exact thoughts."

He gestured into the sunroom, which was all windows and couches that looked like they belonged outside on a patio. They sat on opposite couches and put their drinks on a low glass-topped table. Madison looked like she was choosing her words carefully.

"It's just terrifying to me. Whenever I would lose a client or fall behind in my basic bills I'd think I might become a bag lady if I don't learn to... what? Attract money. Sometimes it even had me catching myself being attracted to a man simply because he had money."

Madison regretted saying that part as soon as it came out of her mouth. What would Robert Chance think of that? Especially because it is so obvious that Chance had money. This seaside property in Santa Monica is not what your average retired cop owns. How did he get it all, anyway? She wondered again. Dare she ask him?

"First of all," said Chance, "you work. Do you understand that? You work for a living, and every day you work your skills improve because you've worked and learned for another day. Your money might not improve day by day but your skills do, so your capacity for earning your way keeps increasing. Whether you know it or not. Whether you like it or not. Nothing you can do about the truth of it."

"Except to deny it," said Madison. "And repress it and be totally unaware of it."

"Right! Which is why the coaching is working for you because coaching removes your denial. It removes the blinders and reveals how capable you really are. The reality of it. Do you really think it's true that you could be a bag lady?"

"I fear it."

"That's not what I'm asking. Do you really think it's true that you might become one? Really and truly?"

"Not when you put it that way."

"I'm not putting it any way. I'm asking a simple question."

"Okay, I guess not."

"Which sounds like a no."

"So why have I been so afraid of it?"

"You believe the picture you have of it without challenging

the picture. Ever. Picture appears, and you go into fear. It's time you knew that you do get to challenge your beliefs. There's a you in there bigger and better than your negative beliefs. If you don't practice challenging everything negative, you just keep on believing a false fairy tale picture of a bag lady."

"I'm feeling strange right now."

"In what way?"

"Somehow I can't make the fear come up. It's like the fear was all in the past. It's funny. This used to happen to me sometimes when I'd go to the doctor. I'd have some problem and I'd wait and wait and it wouldn't go away so I'd finally go see the doctor and when I was finally in the examining room and he would say 'Show me were it hurts,' it wouldn't hurt any more. I couldn't make it hurt. It was embarrassing."

Chance smiled. "You wished you were still hurting!"

Madison laughed. She said, "I was afraid that when I left the clinic they'd be writing the words *acute hypochondria* on my chart."

"I think we need to book an actual coaching session on this," said Chance. "Because there's a second piece to this that you'll enjoy even more."

"Which piece is that?"

"The piece where we find out that even if you *were* a bag lady you could *still* have the time of your life."

"That session may take longer than we have time for."

Chance was smiling, not at her remark, but at the word "MONKEY" on Madison's file folder sitting on the glass table. He tapped his finger on it.

"Very clever," he said. "Not everyone knows a gibbon is a kind of monkey."

"It's called tradecraft. I've read my spy novels. I know who George Smiley is."

"Another example of your skills growing even when you don't know they are. You probably thought you were goofing off reading Le Carré spy books, but look at you now. Everything is practice. Everything supports you, and I mean everything. Reality is much better than we think it is."

"I think we just proved that when you asked if I *really* thought I could be a bag lady."

"We brought it back to reality, and the fear went away."

Madison reached for her MONKEY file as Chance stood up to refresh his coffee. He pointed to her tea and she waved him no. While he was in the kitchen she stood to look out the windows of the sunroom. She wondered about what she was experiencing the past few days. She couldn't remember ever feeling better about just being alive.

Chance came back and sat down. Madison took one more deep breath at the window and sat across from him.

"This is a bad person," said Madison, tapping her finger on the file folder holding her information on Gibbon.

"Well, not really," said Chance. "He's just totally confused."

"Are you still coaching now? Come down from your Zen cloud. Real world, everyday language now. So that we understand each other."

"Okay." Chance smiled. "This Gibbon is a bad guy. Agreed. But how bad? Arson bad or murder bad? Because they are completely different levels of bad."

"We have to be looking at murder bad here because this whole thing started with Tom Dumar dying and you and I both thinking that it could not have been suicide."

"Right. But right now we have arson, and we have a pathetic young guy with gas cans who said he was paid by Gary Gibbon to burn a cabin down."

"And they've got Gary?"

"I'm assuming Gary's in custody waiting to be interviewed by Sergeant Mossi today. I was asked to do it, but I'm just going to observe."

"Won't Gary talk about his dad? Put it on his father?"

"We don't know that. We'll have to see."

"Why haven't they brought in Gibbon himself?"

"They have nothing at all on Gibbon yet, and we want to be careful about giving them what *you've* got in case it might not have been acquired through proper protocol. If you get my meaning."

"I could go to jail."

"You could."

"Would it be worse than being a bag lady?"

"That would be up to you."

35

Brock Young was taking the long walk through the Denver airport noticing that the carpet had a pattern of little airplanes. He hated that. Why do they do that? *Do we have to be reminded that we're in an airport? Do they think we'll forget where we are if we look down at the carpet?*

Brock Young was feeling like he was reverting back to Gibbon again already, hating everything he saw. Why couldn't he have left that behind?

He guessed that the hatred started when he was a teenager and found out that his parents weren't who he wanted them to be. He'd feel it in his temples, throbbing until he couldn't bear it any longer. The church took him in and gave him the sense of control he wanted. Also the leverage, the platform to evaluate other people from. Righteousness and judgment. Like when that guy Chance thought suicide was forgivable. He thought more about Chance and decided that he hated Chance for more than that. It was his confidence. He couldn't sense any fear or hate in Chance and Brock Young hated that fact.

The man who was now Brock Young had been to Denver before. He'd tried, when he was Gibbon, to start some real estate dealings with fellow church members there but nothing worked out. He'd always disliked this airport. It was not even near Denver. It was a stretch to even call it the Denver airport. Wishful naming. The location was so far away that on one of his visits he impulsively completed every meeting on the phone in the cab during the endless drive to the city and then told the driver to turn around and take him back. It took so long for the driver to understand the request that Gibbon exploded in a fury, gave him no tip, and took a different cab back to Denver International.

On his second visit there he decided to simply stay in an airport hotel and meet people there but was angered to discover that even the airport hotel was a full twenty-minute drive away!

When he got off the plane this time he saw that those ugly white tents that made up the roof of the airport were now getting dirty. They looked like Madonna's power-bra concert cones. Even this airport haunted him with reminders of women without class.

That would soon change.

That was his belief now.

He recalled losing his baggage here once. The automated baggage loss system was amazingly unreliable. And once off the plane there was an endless tedious train ride to get to the baggage area. Brock Young fought his feelings of disgust.

Perhaps only a special woman could relieve the anger he felt when he experienced man's architectural stupidity.

Once he took his two large metallic samsonite bags off the baggage carousel he went outside and got in a cab. It was chilly in Denver. He realized he might start to miss California. Because as much as he hated L.A., he hated chilly weather even more.

Brock Young shivered as he read the address of his new home to the driver. The driver nodded. Did the driver understand the address? Did he even understand English? He studied his name on the license above the meter. Incomprehensible name. What if all these guys were placed here by Bin Laden?

Drones wouldn't function here. It would be too late.

36

Madison was speaking softly but it didn't matter how audible she was because no one was there to hear her. Her hands flew across the keyboard of her computer, and although her red nails were stylishly short they clicked as she entered variations on "Glen Gibbon divorce" into her search engine.

Once she'd found the former Mrs. Gibbon, whose former name was Mollie Bee Makem, she found a court document that showed an order for child support, dated before Mollie Bee's wedding date with Glen. So she was married before? Then had a daughter with Gibbon.

More searching and more talking to the screen ("Come on, just come to me, I won't hurt you, come out of hiding... okay, bingo...") and the daughter's name was Carrie. Based on her date of birth Carrie would be fifteen right now. Living with her mother? Her mother was awarded full custody and they've both retaken the maiden name Makem.

Madison rolled her office chair back a few feet and looked out her window. A strange yellowish green bird was visiting the bird feeder. What in the world? It looked like a parakeet.

A parakeet out in the wild?

Well, not exactly the wild, it's just my back yard, but still. How could it be a parakeet? She got up and looked at the bird again. She'd never seen anything like it at her feeder. Someone's parakeet got loose?

She went into her front room where the bookshelves were and pulled her *Sibley Field Guide to Birds of Western North America* from the top shelf. It was the most worn-out book on the shelf. Parakeet. Parakeet. She went through the pages and found a parakeet. No. Doesn't look the same. That's not it. Almost, but not it.

She tiptoed back into her office to look outside again, and, well, yes, good. The bird was still there. She looked more closely at it now. Its face and throat were pinkish, a dark rose color on its forehead. The bill was greenish-yellow, and its legs and feet were grey.

Back to the book. She began thumbing through the whole book page by page. Why was this so important? Somehow everything in her life seemed important now. Or, if not important, maybe just *exciting* in a subtle way... here it is! I found you, you pretty little thing. Oh my goodness, it was an *Agapornis roseicollis* or what is more commonly known as a peach-faced lovebird.

A lovebird outside her window.

She dives into work on this case and a lovebird appears. Was she insane right now to be reading anything into this?

She wanted to email Chance and tell him. Or maybe send a text. But why? He didn't exactly take the bait when she told him that the word *koi* was Japanese for "love and harmony."

But, still, the universe yields clues, does it not? There truly is the existence of unreasonable coincidence and synchronicities. She always believed in that and really it wasn't even a belief. Beliefs you had to try to hang on to.

Like frantic hoping.

This felt more solid.

More like a *realizing*.

She realized, for example, that when she was really enjoying life, living in the flow, or whatever it was, all these coincidences and synchronicities started showing up. Like clues from the universe. But clues to what? That she was on the right path?

Her aunt told her once that coincidence was God winking at you from beyond. From a distance. Like one of her favorite Bette Midler songs. God is watching us… from a distance.

She looked back at her computer screen and then picked up the *Sibley* bird guide to take it back to the bookshelf. Her thoughts went back to her investigation. She was grateful for that. She started to feel more settled.

Where would Carrie Makem be? And she's fifteen, so what could she even know about this case? If her father Glen Gibbon was involved in something, how would she know? In fact, she may never have spent much time with Gibbon.

Madison thought about teenage girls. What were they like these days? Why did they seem so different? Madison remembered a simpler life as a teenage girl. She used to dream of riding in that convertible with Elvis in that old movie *Blue Hawaii*. Or dating Jon Bon Jovi. That was as wild as her fantasies got. Today it's meth and vampires and piercings and a body covered with tattoos. Was this societal evolution?

Just when she had begun to believe that society was going in the wrong direction, her own life was getting dramatically better. More integrity, more creativity. More love. More opportunity to serve people.

It occurred to her that she had a niece a year older than Carrie Makem. Hayley. Hayley was always on her cell phone or else on Facebook or MySpace. Okay. *That's where I will look.* I'll look for Carrie on Facebook and MySpace or Twitter.

There can't be that many Carrie Makems around here.

37

Chance met Mossi in the lobby of the main LAPD headquarters building. They shook hands and Mossi motioned to chairs around a low circular table in the far corner of the lobby. Completely secluded. On the wall were framed pictures of officers who died in the line of duty.

"Let's sit here for a few minutes," Mossi said. "They're going to page me when the prisoner and our conference room are ready for us. Coffee? Water?"

"No. I'm good."

Chance welcomed the opportunity to rest his legs. He'd overdone his workout this morning with his trainer Wu Li and the deep Hindu squats had his thighs burning whenever he stood up. Workouts of this intensity were something Chance thought he'd left behind forever, but something about this case had him fired up. An intuition inside had him wanting to bring his body back to where it was when he was a serious cop.

A coach's body wasn't going to match up with the challenge he felt was in front of him. He didn't know if that was actually true, but it felt good to behave as if it was.

"Have you been to the scene of the fire?" said Chance, as the two men sat.

Mossi looked around the lobby and pulled his chair up close to the round glass table and Chance. "That Canyon gives me the creeps," Mossi said. "Usually I don't go in for things like the Bermuda Triangle, ghosts, past lives... any of that... but I can't drive into Laurel Canyon without feeling something. You know what I'm talking about?"

"I think it's a great place," said Chance. "A deep lush canyon, trees and brush and houses and cabins built into the hillsides. A little crazy, of course. And you have to love the Country Store."

"No, I don't have to love it," said Mossi. "That store is often the meeting place for all kinds of bad characters."

"And the history there is amazing. All the great musicians who have lived there. Got their initial inspiration there."

"And died there, don't forget that," said Mossi. "The music died in that canyon a long time ago. I lost my sense of enchantment when Wonderland happened. I worked the fringes of that case, and it made me never want to go into the canyon again."

Chance knew Wonderland, too. He'd been brought in years later to help with a follow-up interrogation. He was new to the force, barely out of the academy, but the brutality of the murders on 8763 Wonderland Avenue shook him up and made him immediately reconsider police work. The bloody palm print of porn star John Holmes at the scene with four bludgeoned corpses ought to have made the case fairly simple but Chance got to see how badly a case could unravel. Once the teams of powerful defense lawyers began feeding its complexity it looked like it would go on forever.

"Wonderland was unique," said Chance. "Nothing like it since Manson's so-called children did their killing sprees twelve years earlier."

"No, not unique," Mossi said. "Tip of the freaking Laurel Canyon iceberg. That canyon is cursed. I could tell you more cases than you want to hear about. Even music people who eventually died premature deaths elsewhere had homes in Lauren Canyon. Jimi Hendrix. Jim Morrison. Mama Cass. Gram Parsons. Tim Buckley. Phil Ochs. Plus numerous other lesser-known music people there who died drug-related violent deaths."

"What does that have to do with our case?"

"The whole place is cursed. That fire could have had a hundred different motivating factors. Drugs, pornography, insurance, sexual healing."

"Sexual healing?"

"Revenge. I call it sexual healing. Love triangles that damage the male ego beyond repair."

"I understand the history. But I like the canyon. Graham Nash's song *Our House* was about his house in Laurel Canyon. That's the canyon I know."

"That exact house burned to the ground!" said Mossi as he grabbed his vibrating cell phone, looked at the text, and then clapped it shut. "Conference room is ready for us. And that house of Nash's burned to the ground."

"I heard you the first time. But I like the canyon anyway. Simply because I do. And it helps me focus."

"How so?"

"On the offensiveness of this particular fire. It helps me to not see it as a part of a haunted history, but something unique unto itself that never should have happened. A brutal affront to the social contract we all have with each other."

"Whatever," said Mossi. "No wonder you got out of police work. No cop could understand you."

"Then I'll simplify it. You don't burn my friend's house down and get away with it."

Mossi stared at Chance. Something about his tone of voice made him shift his opinion a little. Maybe he was a cop's cop after all.

38

Chance and Detective Mossi moved into the conference room for their pre-interview strategy session. Mossi had a can of Diet Dr. Pepper and Chance was drinking hot water from a coffee cup. He wasn't against the strategic use of caffeine, but he had a limit.

Mossi said, "You seem to know more about this Gary Gibbon than I do so why don't you do the talking first?"

"No, it's yours. But you can talk to him about what I told you I know. He'll know what you say is true because I'll be sitting right there for him to see. I may even nod a little when you speak."

"Whatever happened to good cop, bad cop?"

"Let's start with us both being good. We can always switch later."

"What do you really know about this punk? Rico Hornsby said he was paid by him... a thousand dollars to do the fire. Actually two thousand. Anything else we know?"

"He followed me in traffic. I was going to visit the widow of your suicide victim Tom Dumar, shortly after the incident. I was going to see her at the very cabin that burned down, and I saw that he was following me."

"Are you sure it was him?"

"Quite sure."

"How did you know?"

"I have my ways of knowing things like this. One of them is

looking at a man's face point blank. Another is writing a license plate number down. Secret techniques like that. We don't have time to talk about all of it. Let's see what we can find out."

"Where do you think the motive is here? No one was home. And the insurance was in the name of Dumar and his wife. So where does this guy come in?"

"I bet you'll find out."

"Just ask him if his father is an alcoholic?"

"You'll know what to ask. You've done this a lot."

"But not like you did. I tend to do things logically. You went illogical on me with that gas can kid."

"Ready to go?"

Mossi straightened his belt and stood up. He and Chance put their can and cup away and left the conference room and headed for the interrogation room.

 **39**

Gary Gibbon had an orange jail jumpsuit on and was sitting straight upright as Mossi and Chance watched him through the video monitor in the hall. A uniformed guard stood outside the door pretending not to listen to the detective and the ex-detective observe the subject.

"Looks like he's a student eager for school," said Mossi with an amused sense of surprise in his voice.

"Yes, this could be a tricky one," said Chance.

Mossi nodded for the guard to open the door to let both men in.

"Gary Gibbon?" said Mossi, as Gary stood up. "I'm Sergeant Mossi and this is my partner Robert Chance who is working as a consultant on the case."

Gary's eyes were on Chance the whole time Mossi spoke.

"Gary, have you been read your rights?" Mossi said.

Gary nodded yes.

"Please sit down, son. We just have a few questions for you. You know you can have an attorney if you want one."

Gary nodded yes.

"Is that yes you want an attorney, or yes you know your rights?" said Mossi.

"Yes I know my rights," said Gary.

"Good. Now, Gary, why don't you tell Mr. Chance and me what it is you do for a living."

"I work for my father."

"And what kind of work is that?"

"He's in real estate. So I do all kinds of things. I help fix up houses and things like that."

"How old are you, Gary?"

"Twenty-two."

"And how long have you been working for your father?"

"All my life."

"Gary, do you know anything about that fire they had in Laurel Canyon two days ago?"

"No, sir. Well, I saw it on the news; that's all."

"So that was the extent of it for you? You know any of the people whose houses burned down?"

"Not that I know of."

"Do you know of a guy named Rico Hornsby?"

Something shifted behind Gary's eyes when he heard the name, and he sat up in his chair even straighter than before.

"I don't think so. I don't know. I hire a lot of guys with names like that. Rico. I hire 'em by the hour to help me fix up my dad's houses. I don't remember that name. Maybe I know him but I don't think so."

"So you might know him, you might not," said Mossi. "I can certainly understand that if you hire a lot of people."

Chance could see that Mossi had decided to go "good cop" with Gary. But he could also see that it wasn't a totally natural thing for him. There was something pent up in Mossi that wanted to get out. Mossi was nodding his head and forcing a tight smile as if everything Gary was saying was understandable. Like it all made sense. Like maybe this was just a simple misunderstanding! This orange suit you were in, maybe it wasn't necessary. Maybe we could get you out of those cuffs, too, after a few more simple questions.

Body language worked both ways. Chance had often seen detectives demonstrate more closed-off, uncomfortable body language than the suspects themselves. Suspects see it too. And Mossi's body language was exhibiting strain and stress.

"Gary," said Mossi, "you say you hire guys to help you."

"Yes, sir."

"What would you pay a guy, say a guy like Rico Hornsby if he helped you?"

"I didn't say I did. I didn't say I knew Rico. I just said I hired guys with names like his so I might have… but I don't know."

"Okay, Gary, I understand. So let's just say anybody. Any average guy you would hire to help you fix a house. What would you pay him? Say for two hours' work."

"I'm not sure. It would depend."

Chance could see a small vein starting to throb on Mossi's neck. He saw Mossi's hand tighten around his pen. It was like watching the Coke can in Chance's back yard explode that unusually hot summer day a year ago. A client had left it there in the July heat after an outdoor session. It wasn't opened and the next day Chance looked out his window as it rolled off the picnic table. The aluminum was stretched and the can was bulging and looked like an aluminum blimp. When it hit the ground it exploded, Coke spraying all around.

Mossi said, "Gary, are you saying you're not sure what you pay people?"

"Not always. Not exactly."

"Because I'm not buying that, Gary. Okay?"

"You're not buying what?"

"That you don't know what you pay people."

"It varies."

"Of course. But to help you fix up a house, you would be able to tell me right off what you paid a character like Rico Hornsby. Unless you were just being a little difficult here. A little stingy with the truth."

"I'm telling you what I know."

"And I'm not buying that you are. Okay with you that I'm not buying that?"

"I guess so."

"Because, *of course you're sure* what you pay people. Everybody knows what they pay people, Gary. That includes you. Money's important to all of us, isn't it Gary? Isn't that why they call it money?"

Gary said nothing. It looked like he was closing his eyes and then he opened them wider than they've ever been opened in his life when Mossi's fist slammed down on the table causing both Gary and Chance to jump.

"How about a thousand dollars, Gary?!!" Mossi was screaming. "How about a thousand dollars now and a thousand dollars after!! Does that jog your memory? Cause that's what I hear you're paying people these days!"

Mossi stood up and said, "Hell, Gary, can I work for you?! I'll start right now. Can I work for you, Gary? I could use a thousand now and a thousand later!"

Chance put a hand on Mossi's forearm and felt all the muscles jumping. After a few seconds he removed his hand and all was silent. Mossi sat down.

Finally, Gary said in a shaking whisper, "I want an attorney. I won't answer another question without one."

40

Chance looked like he was trying not to laugh out loud as he looked through the box of donuts in the conference room after the interrogation of Gary Gibbon.

He found the last plain donut and took a bite. He finally turned to Mossi and said, "Nice job."

"Yeah, right."

"Have you ever thought about anger management?"

Mossi was munching on a white powdered donut and looking at Chance to see if he was kidding.

"I despise kids like that," said Mossi. "And I *know* I blew it. Pushed him into the arms of his attorney."

"No, it was fine. I said it would be tricky anyway, and I don't think he was going to give us anything no matter what we did. I'm not bothered about him. Actually it's you I'm concerned about."

"Why?"

"Because you stress yourself out—that's not going to be good for you over the long haul. I know you're a good cop, but stress isn't the same as being committed and dedicated. You can relax and still do great work."

Mossi gestured toward the coffee machine and Chance smiled and shook his head no. Mossi tried to find his words.

"Listen," said Mossi, "it's not that complicated. I'm pretty much of an old-school guy. I'm not sensitive like today's cops. These young detectives are all about their feelings and plugging in to the internet today."

"It's called keeping up with the world."

"They're always focused on the internet and cell phones. They're going over everyone's cell phone records to see who called who. They even know how to tell where the callers were when they called. Something to do with towers."

Chance said, "I've got a client who's helping me look into this case who knows all that high tech stuff. I'm for whatever works. Nothing modern about murder, but there's also nothing wrong with old-fashioned detective work."

"There you go again with murder," said Mossi. "We're a long way away from murder in this deal. You were life coaching this guy Dumar, and he killed himself and somehow you can't accept it. I admit, there's *something* going on here, and I'm okay that you're helping me. Really, truly am. But let's not lose our heads."

"Well, okay, and by the way, I've never liked the term life coaching. I rarely call it that myself. I work with people. I work on their problems or whatever they want a second pair of eyes to see. I get results, or, rather *they* get results. Life coaching sounds too limited for what I really do."

"You don't coach the whole life of the person?"

"I coach a simple specific problem and then the person, by learning to solve it on their own, becomes more whole. Usually the one problem is a version of all the other problems. Solve the one and the others fall into place."

"Okay, tell me this, then, wise one. What's *my* problem?"

Chance reached for another plain donut. They were gone. He shrugged his shoulders and his face softened as he read Mossi's eyes. Was Mossi being truly open right now or just testing the waters?

"I don't see a problem," said Chance. "You yourself would have to see a problem for there to be a problem."

"No, you said anger. You asked if I had considered anger management. So don't say you don't see a problem. Don't do your Gandhi thing with me when you know damn well I've got a problem."

"Okay. How *are* you with anger management… in your own opinion?"

"I don't know whether they had this when you were a cop, but they actually have a program for that now. A police shrink works with you. I've done a couple sessions. Ridiculous. Worthless. "

"But is your anger a problem to *you*?"

"I don't know. It never feels great. How would I know?"

"Well. Answer this. Do you *do* your anger like an actor would? Or does it do you?"

"Or what?"

"Or does it control *you*? Does it seem to have a life of its own?"

"It comes out of nowhere."

Chance's eyes began to twinkle. He nodded. He tried not to smile.

"That's funny?" said Mossi. "I'm telling you things I never told anyone except my mother and you try not to laugh?"

"I'm just happy to hear that it feels like it comes from nowhere. Because the next step is easy. You question it until you see that it comes from somewhere specific… some thought you have. You can question it like you question a suspect."

"Treat my thought like a suspect."

"Right. Thoughts should all be suspect. Especially the negative ones."

"Well, I'm not too interested in all this anyway," said Mossi getting up and stretching his arms over his head. "I'm not interested in making this be all about me. I've got work to do. I talk with *you* long enough and I'll be going home to watch *Oprah* on my lunch break."

"Wouldn't want that to happen," said Chance.

Mossi was trying to decide whether to feel bad or good as the two men stood up to shake hands and say good bye. He called out to Chance.

"I'm going to have one of my young guys check cell records on Gary Gibbon and Hornsby, et cetera. We'll go back in when he gets his attorney. We'll still be moving this thing right along."

"I know you will. It was a good thing, today. Don't feel bad about today."

"How was it good?"

"You got him an attorney."

"And how's that good?"

"He really needs one."

41

Marquis Boston was a private investigator who also ran ads on the internet making himself available for "career counseling" to those who were looking to begin a life in investigation.

People like Madison Kerr.

His office was in downtown L.A. next to Our Lady of the Angels cathedral on Temple Street between Grand Avenue and Figueroa. Madison's trip up the elevator to Boston's office was a mixture of fear and positive excitement. Once she'd found Gibbon's daughter Carrie on MySpace and saw the school she attended and the places she liked to hang out, she knew there were now things she wanted to do that went far beyond internet searching.

Boston's assistant was a young black woman who looked like she'd just won a TV reality show for runway modeling. She took Madison's name and smiled and asked her to take a seat in the reception area. Framed photos of Marquis Boston with police chiefs and celebrities surrounded the soft, deep cushioned maroon and gold reception chairs. A very large photo of Boston and Phil Spector was in the center of the others. Boston looked like a young Sidney Poitier. *They call me MISTER Boston,* thought Madison.

The assistant picked up her phone and spoke softly to whoever called, though there was no ring or buzz. She hung up and stood up and walked around her desk toward Madison.

"Mr. Boston will see you now, Miss Kerr," she said as she led Madison to a door with a large gold star on it and the word "Boston" engraved inside the star.

Madison wondered just how credible this private eye was.

"Come in, Madelyn, is it?" said a booming voice from a desk by a huge picture window far into the office.

"Madison," said the receptionist as she closed the door. Madison looked at a smiling Marquis Boston seated behind a huge desk. He gestured for her to take the chair in front of the desk.

"You noticed the star on the door?" said Boston, who was dressed in a black suit with grey pinstripes and a bright pink shirt open at the collar. Madison thought he may have been wearing the exact costume Luther Van Dross was wearing at the concert she and her father saw six years ago at the Staples Center.

"Yes, I noticed the star," she said. "It looks like Hollywood's sidewalk of fame."

"That was the point," said Boston, chuckling. "It was given to me by Yoko Ono. I did some work for her once. That's the beauty of L.A. When you're good at what you do around here, you get the attention of every celebrity in the world."

"It must be exciting for you," said Madison, in a voice that told him it wasn't actually all that exciting for her.

"Oh, no. People are just people. You get used to it." He gestured to a bar by the wall to her left. "Something to drink?"

"No, I'd like to use the time I've purchased to find out about this line of work."

"Absolutely!" said Boston. "This is the best business in the world to start on your own, especially now. The private investigator has risen in status now that we're in the information age. Years ago we were considered fairly shady, but now we're in demand."

"What sort of work do you do the most of?"

"Missing persons, hidden assets, developing cases for trial. That kind of thing. Love, too. We can't leave out love." His eyes twinkled as he made a tent with his fingers while looking at Madison's legs recently tanned by the beach.

"Love?" she said, sitting up straighter and smoothing down her beige skirt.

"Well, yes," said Boston, clearing his throat and snapping into businesslike mode. He glanced out his picture window. "What's love got to do with it? Divorce! Infidelity. That kind of thing. That category goes way back. I remember my first cases were for upset husbands and wives, back when it was basic. No internet snooping back then. No internet! We went through trash cans ourselves. With our bare hands. Especially the days right after Valentine's Day. That was always the best time to look."

Madison took out her notebook. She took out her pen and looked down at the list of questions she'd made that morning. She didn't know why the infidelity subject made her so uncomfortable.

"Mr. Boston, how do private investigators handle it when they're working on an active case that the police also have? Say, an arson or murder case."

"We do great work in those situations," he said, "or at least I do. My firm. Because of the computer, there are people in private life, civilians, who do far better than law enforcement now in many cases. I have a young partner, Sandy Redfield, who does that side of things for me. He's like my own personal surfer dude who works out of his home. The FBI just hired us to train a new class of agents on the latest forms of computer tracking."

"That's impressive," said Madison.

"You'd be surprised at the people who hire us. You know our number one source of revenue last quarter?"

"Government?" guessed Madison.

"No, other private investigators. They get stuck, hit a brick wall, and need to deliver so they call me and I put surfer dude on it and it's done. He can find things no one else can find Like hidden money off shore. And missing persons. And now that the banking industry has been found out to be less than trustworthy, there's a lot of upset investors out there. It's a field day for us."

Madison went through all the questions on her list. She asked them one by one. Boston took his time with each answer, and the more he talked the more Madison respected him. There was a lot more to him than the flashy first impression he made. Some of her questions were about the internet and Boston's answer to each of those was, "Surfer dude. You'd be better off asking him that one."

Finally, as her hour was coming to a finish, she asked Boston if surfer dude would talk to her. She'd be glad to pay for it.

"Not normally," said Boston. "He's not that into this kind of thing. Human relations are not his strongest suit. He is a very private guy. But he'll do it if I tell him to. And I think he'll be glad I sent *you*." Boston smiled a knowing smile at Madison as she stood to leave.

"Where would I find him?"

"In the water," said Boston laughing. "At least during the day. But his card's up front with Tangela. Sandy Redfield is his name. Call his cell. His number is on the card. Pre-pay Tangela for your time with him, if you want. And I'll tell him you're calling."

"Thank you, sir."

Madison left realizing that she liked Mr. Boston a lot more at the end than at the beginning. He was bright and funny and very helpful. It made her feel even better about this work that she was venturing into.

 **42**

Brian "Sandy" Redfield had a Venice Beach apartment just two blocks from Santa Monica. All the windows inside had an ocean view. Madison stood inside and looked around. With the sun going down over the water, she never remembered seeing anything so beautiful from an apartment.

Sandy was making her a green tea and banana smoothie as she stepped out onto the porch looking out over the water. The waves were crashing in, and each crash somehow made her feel more intrigued by this line of work.

Sandy brought the smoothies out to the porch and motioned for Madison to sit down. He had a huge shock of red-blond hair and a sunburned nose and forehead. He looked to Madison to be not a day over twenty, but she knew she was probably wrong about that. He had a powder blue tee shirt on that had a red rectangular robot's head on it with yellow eyes and the words BAD ROBOT underneath. His arms were tanned and muscular and he seemed to not be able to stop smiling at her.

"Mr. Boston said I'd like you," said Sandy, "and he was right."

"I haven't said anything."

"True," said Sandy. "That's cool, too."

Madison wondered if this would be a really a good use of her time. But she was already there and maybe she could learn something.

"How long have you been doing this work?"

"About three years," said Sandy. "I did it part time for Mr. Boston a couple of years before that."

"Do you have to have a license to do what you do?" Madison was peeking back through the open porch doors into the main living room that had a desk that spanned the whole wall with four computer screens and other electronic set-ups on it.

"I finally got one by getting a degree online," said Sandy. "You're supposed to have three years investigative experience, but if you have a degree it can be less. You looking to do that?"

"I may be. What kind of degree would I want?"

"Police science. Have you done any college?"

"I have a degree in business administration."

"You can fly through police science online."

Madison was taking notes when she heard a strange sound from a distant room inside the apartment. It sounded like small explosions but they were being made by a small human voice. She turned her head to the noise and then back to Sandy, who shrugged and smiled.

"My son," he said. "That's Ben. He's got his superhero action figures engaged in battle again."

Madison smiled. She had a nephew who played violent video games that his father, her brother, actually approved of. Said it taught him superior hand-eye coordination and tuned up his brain synapses. She never knew if she agreed.

"Do all boys like that kind of thing?" she said in the friendliest voice she could find.

"His mother, who lives in Minnesota, doesn't think he should be so obsessed. Thinks I should give him little animals and furry figures to play with… teach him to enjoy houseplants. But I loved my G.I. Joe stuff when I was little. I think it's in our blood. A quest for the heroic is not always a bad thing."

More explosions came from Ben's room followed by, "Dush, dush, dush, aaaah! No, no!"

"Well, okay," said Madison. "What would count as experience toward a private investigator's license for me?"

"Any investigation you are doing for law enforcement, insurance fraud investigators, or another private eye, as long as it's compensated."

"How about work done for an ex-cop who's consulting on a case for the LAPD?"

"That would count. Log your hours. Keep your time diary. And be liberal and generous. Time spent thinking counts for the license application, as far as I'm concerned. I even put down some time I spent dreaming. I kept a dream journal."

Madison liked him.

There was something totally unaffected about how he kept smiling. It was the opposite of Glen Gibbon's automatic switch-on, switch-off phony smile. This smile just seemed to come over Sandy without him knowing it was coming.

"Are you working on something now?" he said.

"Yes. It's complicated. A suicide that has turned into arson. And there have been many mysterious points in between."

"That Laurel Canyon fire?" said Sandy.

"That may be involved, yes," said Madison, now wondering if she should be saying anything about this.

"Did you know Mama Cass's old cabin was burned down in that fire?" said Sandy. "That really upset me. Laurel Canyon was the birthplace of the coolest music in the world for a while there. Frank Zappa. Stephen Stills. Neil Young."

"I know that, and it's a shame."

"Fats Domino," said Sandy, smiling again.

"Fats Domino lived in Laurel Canyon? I thought he was New Orleans…"

"No, no," said Sandy. "'Ain't That a Shame,' Fats Domino sang 'Ain't That a Shame.'"

Madison wasn't all that interested in musical history, but the word shame lingered in her mind. She said, "How much of that is there in this work?"

"How much of what?"

"You know, shame. Shame and sadness and just bummer stuff."

"It won't bother you after a while. You'll love what you do if you get into this, especially if you are into the internet and know that world, which Mr. Boston said was why you wanted to talk to me."

"Is there any down side?"

"It's just all cool. There is no down side, except maybe one caution."

"And that would be?"

"Attorneys. Most private investigators do work for defense attorneys and that can get on the depressing side."

"How do you mean?"

"Anything for money. No right or wrong. No truth, justice, and the American way. You can feel less than awesome after that kind of work. Discrediting good people so your attorney's criminal can get off. Not that much fun."

"And Mr. Boston doesn't do much of that?"

"He did work for Johnny Cochran when Johnny was alive, but that was about it. And with the exception of O.J., Mr. Cochran had a good moral compass."

Again from the bedroom, "Dush, dush! Oh. Aaaack! You're dead! Oh, no I'm NOT!"

Sandy looked at Madison for minute, amused at her slightly raised eyebrows as the sounds of a superhero Armageddon came out to the porch. He said, "I care a lot about the Byrds, *Sweetheart of the Rodeo* and all of that," he said.

Is this guy insane? Is he high on something? She gave him a look that said, "Tell me what you mean."

"I mean, the Byrds got their start in Laurel Canyon, too," he said. "And I was upset by that fire."

"And so?"

"And so I just tracked some things and fooled with it a little."

"In what way?"

"I've built up some sources over the years. Chat room friends you might say. Sources."

"And?"

"And there was a resident of a cabin in that fire who tried to get extra insurance about a month ago."

"Who was that?"

"Let me look again because I took it down," said Sandy motioning Madison into the living room. The sun had begun to go down over the water and he turned on two overhead lights and went through a pile of papers on the floor by his office chair. He found the one he was looking for.

"Tom Dumar," he said.

Madison tried to make sense of that. It would take time to think that through. Not here. Not now. She said, "Well, maybe we can talk again some time."

Sandy's son Ben was standing in the open door to his bedroom holding two action figures in his hands.

"Dad?" he said.

"Ben this is Miss...Miss Madison."

"Oh," said Ben. "Dad?"

"Ben, what do you say?"

"Hello," said Ben.

Madison walked over to Ben and said hello and shook the little hand that still contained Spider-Man.

Ben said, "Dad, does Spider-Man have any super powers? Like x-ray vision like Superman?"

"No," said Sandy.

"That sucks for him," said Ben.

"No it doesn't," said Sandy, "because he doesn't need them. He's taught himself to do all kinds of things with webs and ropes and stuff. That's what makes him so great."

"Whatever," said Ben. "But Superman could kill him real easy."

"He could but he wouldn't," said Sandy.

"Why not?" said Ben.

"Because they're both good. They're on the same side."

Ben went back into his room. There were fresh new cries of, "Dush! Dush! Aaah! I'm caught in a web! Aaaaa!"

Madison smiled and went to the door and turned to shake Sandy's hand.

"Being on the good side is still important, isn't it?" she said to Sandy.

"Yes, it is! It's everything. If I can help you with whatever you're doing, let me know."

"It's really extraordinary of you to do that," she said, just now noticing two guitars and a small keyboard in the far corner of the room.

"You don't just burn down Mama Cass's house and have me be cool with it. Mama Cass was an earth mother in the Canyon. She gave so many of those musicians shelter and encouragement. Especially the Byrds."

He was smiling but he was serious. Madison knew she could call him again and feel good about it. It felt like he was on her side, and who knew... maybe they were not all that much unlike Spider-Man and Superman.

■ ■ ■

"Tom Dumar took extra insurance out on the cabin," Madison said into Robert Chance's voice mail as she drove out from Venice Beach past Marina Del Rey toward her own house. "Call me ASAP."

The drive home was exhilarating for Madison. She opened her windows and let the moist ocean breezes throw her hair around and curl it up. She looked forward to talking to Chance about taking an online police science curriculum and getting a P.I. license of her own.

She then began to wonder about her desire to visit Carrie Makem, Gibbon's daughter. What could she possibly learn? She didn't know, but she knew she was good with teenage girls. And she had a feeling that women, even young ones, knew more family secrets than men did.

They saw more, heard more, and felt more.

She couldn't prove that was true, but that had been her experience. *We can often get to the bottom of things in ways that men can't.*

Was that reverse sexism? Madison didn't care. She would try to see Carrie and see where that went.

43

Susan Dumar's sister's house in Santa Barbara was about an hour's drive from Chance's last coaching client of the day. His client owned a restaurant in Pacific Palisades and was losing money every month. Chance's coaching was focused on the owner's use of time. All day and night were spent solving problems and resolving employee disputes. There was no focus on the customer.

"What you focus on grows," Chance had told him in the final five minutes of the session. "Focus on your problems and you'll just get more and more problems. Focus on your customers and you'll get more of those."

Chance had helped him set up a secret shopper project in which various people unknown to the employees would come to the restaurant and dine there and later fill out reports on how they were treated, and how they felt about every aspect of their experience.

"If people feel good somewhere and enjoy their experience thoroughly, they will come back. And they will bring other people in," Chance had said. "Let's become obsessive about that process and watch how fast all your other problems go away."

Chance thought back on that coaching session as he went along the highway to Susan Dumar's sister's house.

You get what you focus on.

Chance was focused on finding a solution. Not for closure but for aesthetic completion. Not for revenge but for a cosmic reckoning.

How would he be coaching Susan Dumar right now if he were a grief counselor? What would that so-called "death coach" do? He wasn't sure. Susan had said she called one. But he wasn't even sure whether grief was a problem for Susan. She hadn't stopped the cremation. She seemed to reverse herself on whether Tom's death was a suicide.

Mossi must have a lot of these answers in his investigation files and Chance wasn't ready to press him yet. He was taking Mossi one slow step at a time. He actually liked Mossi now and understood the pressures he was under to close cases and move on.

But he liked Tom Dumar, too, and wanted to honor him with some fact-finding.

Something about that whole death coach joking didn't feel right now. Chance didn't know why. But he'd learned to trust and process every bad feeling that came up, and this was one.

He pulled over into an empty strip mall parking lot. He found his phone in the side pocket of the car door and called Madison. She answered.

Without saying who he was he said, "Can you get to your computer right now?"

"I'm already here," she said.

"Will you look into something called a 'death coach'?"

"Like Susan Dumar told you she called?"

"Right. Yes."

"Call you back in five minutes."

"Good."

"Just one thing," said Madison.

"Yes?"

"Who is this?"

Chance laughed and hung up. He decided to wait in the parking lot and think a bit.

He thought about his first days after the police academy and how proud he was to be a cop. He would walk through the streets and feel like everyone he saw, every man woman and child, was counting on him to keep them safe. It multiplied the experience of being alive. He enjoyed the new consulting and coaching work, but working this case was waking something up again that he hadn't realized was asleep.

His cell rang.

"Find anything?" he said.

"Yes," said Madison. "All the references to death coaches and death coaching were *not* about helping people through the stages of grief!"

"What were they about?"

"They were about helping people to die."

"How do you mean?"

"Just what I said. Assisted suicide, helpful techniques, we death coaches help you help people die."

"Thank you. I'm on my way to see the grieving widow right now. I'll let you know how it goes."

44

The light was on above the front door of Susan's sister's modest white frame house in Santa Barbara. Chance parked across the street. He got out of his car, crossed the street and opened the green picket fence gate, walked up the sidewalk and climbed the steps to the front door.

He knocked.

Susan herself answered and put her fingers to her lips. "Baby's just gone to sleep," she said. "Can we go somewhere?"

Chance said, "Of course," and he and Susan walked to his car.

"There's a tavern four blocks from here and it should be private," she said. "You look stressed, Robert. Shouldn't I be the one who's stressed?"

"In a logical world, you would be."

Susan looked at him with a guarded expression. She turned her attention back to the road ahead.

"This is all very confusing to me," she said. "I just don't feel like I belong anywhere anymore. I'm thinking of moving to Canada. Robert, would you blame me for that? I have friends there who love it and I could be a bookkeeper there or do some office job."

Chance said nothing.

He slowed the car down after the fourth block and Susan said, "On the left. Right here. The Rooster Tail."

Chance parked and they went inside. The tavern was large and dimly lit with sawdust on the floor and a few round tables in the center of the room with booths along the wall. The music system was playing "Who Are You?" by The Who and Susan motioned toward a booth in the corner. Chance said, "Looks good."

Susan ordered a glass of merlot and Chance bourbon on the rocks. They took a moment to relax into the huge booth and to adjust to the pulsing beat of The Who.

Who are you?

When the drinks arrived Chance proposed a toast, "To the memory of Tom," he said, and he noticed Susan's eyes welling up with tears which didn't stop him from adding, "and to the truth about Tom."

Susan said, "Amen" in a voice that didn't mean it.

"I used to wonder what 'Amen' really meant," said Chance.

"I think it means *I'll drink to that*," and she raised her glass of wine again and drank.

"It comes from the Aramaic and it means sealed in faith, trust, and truth," said Chance.

"Sealed in faith, trust, and truth. Not a lot of wiggle room in that. I'm not sure if I like that much finality."

"I don't blame you. So, are you okay talking about Tom?"

"It's probably a good thing to do. Don't you think?"

"Yes, I do. Helps you process things. Tell me about the interment and the services."

"This Sunday the service is at Our Lady of Carmel. You got the email?"

"Yes, I'll be there."

"And we're doing the interment at the lake behind the church. There's a dock there that Tom used to go sit on with me when we wanted to talk things through."

"And the cremation took place against your wishes?"

"Oh, no, Robert, I know I told you I'd make sure they didn't do that, but everything happened so fast and Tom's family was coming to town—his stepparents—and I just caved in to the pressure. I knew you'd be disappointed, but I think we should all just accept it that Tom is gone and he left by his own choosing."

"Why do you think he did that, Susan?"

"He was depressed, as you know; life wasn't really working for him."

"I have to say that was not my experience." Chance stirred his drink with his plastic swizzle stick. There was a rooster at the tip of the stick.

"He wanted to impress you," said Susan. "He always looked up to you. He wanted you to think the coaching was successful. He didn't want you to see the side of him I saw."

"What side was that?"

"Oh, Robert, I don't want to go into it. It's not necessary. Why don't we all move on? You included."

"And the fire? Just move on from that, too?"

"Well, no, I mean we have to find out… or the police have to find out who did that. I have my own ideas about that."

"Have they talked to you?"

"Once for about an hour and I have to go in tomorrow again with my lawyer. They said they have someone in custody."

"What ideas did you have?"

"Tom's enemy. His partner. That Glen Gibbon."

"Did you know Gibbon?"

"I may have met him once."

"Why would *he* do it? Start a fire."

"Probably some house near ours that he owned. He was in real estate. Shady deals. That's all I can think of."

"Were Tom's records in the cabin at home? I didn't see his computer in his office when I looked there."

"Who knows what he kept in his home office? I never went in there."

Chance thought back to how quickly Susan had found Tom's extra set of office keys in his office—for someone who never went in there.

Chance said, "So you didn't bring his computer home?"

"I never went to his office. I couldn't bear it. No. I don't know anything about the computer."

"It seemed like someone scrubbed the office clean. And the gun they found with his body?"

"He must have bought that somewhere."

"Tom hated guns and didn't even want them around. He didn't believe in them And said he had other ways to deal with intruders. So I was surprised that he used a gun."

"Robert, what's the use of all this? You were a cop once, I know that, but you're not a cop anymore. If Tom's parents and if I can accept this, why can't you?"

"I think you may be right," said Chance. He took a long drink of his bourbon. He signaled to the bartender to bring the bill.

"One last question?" said Chance. "Just to get it out of my system."

"Of course," said Susan, placing her hand on Chance's wrist and letting her eyes soften.

"Why, if you only met him once, briefly, do you think Glen Gibbon would have pictures of you on his computer?"

Susan withdrew her hand. She pushed her empty wine glass to the center of the table.

"How would I possibly know the answer to that question?"

Chance shrugged. He waited.

Susan said, "And I'll also tell you this. I don't *want* to know the answer to that question. Do you know what grieving is like, Robert? It's something you want to keep pure and simple. You don't need weird things entering into it. Gibbon was weird. Even sick, the way he treated Tom. You know that more than anyone. You helped get him out of Tom's life. I don't need to explain Gibbon to you."

Chance nodded and put bills on the table to cover the drinks and tip. He and Susan left the Rooster Tail Tavern and drove back to her sister's house in silence. Chance walked her to the door and they gave each other a tentative hug.

"See you at the church Sunday?" said Susan.

"Wouldn't miss it."

■ ■ ■

The ride home from Santa Barbara was less troubled than Chance thought it would be. He was now sure that Susan knew more than she was saying, to say the least. The key here was the suicide. Suicide doesn't usually sit well with people. They can't accept it. They don't make a quick and easy peace with it. Yet Susan seemed to be going in the opposite direction of that. She *wanted* Tom's death to be suicide, over and done with.

Most people want another explanation. Crave it, even. Not only to relieve their own guilt *(Could I have helped more? Could I have done something?)* but it also feels better to think maybe it was accidental or worse.

Maybe their loved one *wasn't* in that much psychological pain.

Maybe someone else even had something to do with it.

Susan also seemed strangely unaffected by the fire that burned her home down. Too ready to move to Canada, as if the fire were just another leaf falling from a tree in the canyon. She was way too ready to move on.

There was too much easy closure happening in her life, and it was happening too quickly. Chance never liked the whole idea of closure, and on this ride home he deepened his determination not to allow any more closure to occur for Susan Dumar if he could help it.

45

Madison Kerr had found Gibbon's daughter Carrie Makem on an internet social site and saw that she had bright red hair and freckles and loved to "hang out" at Venice Beach and skateboard there.

Madison still had an urge to go talk to her but didn't know exactly why. She didn't want to tell Chance it was "intuition" because she was being paid to do serious investigation now.

She sat at her computer and stared at Carrie's face. She looked at the photos of her friends and saw a world that seemed to cover the whole spectrum from gothic to *High School Musical*. It must be so hard to be young in this world.

She imagined how she would do it if she were a teenager right now. No piercings, that was for sure. But could she be sure?

She decided to call Chance.

She walked into her bedroom and flopped down on her queen-sized bed and pushed aside two stuffed animals.

"You there?" she said.

"I'm driving home," said Chance. "Just had a conversation with the grieving widow."

"How is the grieving widow?"

"Not grieving."

"Are you sure? What did you find out?"

"I'll tell you more tomorrow. Can you meet at ten?"

"I'll be there at ten. But can I ask you something now?"

"Ask away."

"Can I interview people?"

"In what way?"

"In my investigation of Gibbon, can I find people and talk to them?"

"Of course you can."

"But I don't have a license or anything as an investigator."

"But you're working for me, and I have one, so you are fine."

"You have a P.I. license?"

"Yes."

"I thought you were just an ex-cop who went right into coaching."

"I took the exam and got my license right after I left the force. Just in case."

"Just in case of what?"

"Just in case someone I was coaching turned up dead under suspicious circumstances."

"Boy, you have amazing foresight."

"Thank you. See you tomorrow."

Madison snapped her phone shut and pulled her white stuffed tiger from the pillow and hugged it to her chest. It reminded her of Siegfried and Roy and the gift shop where her old boyfriend bought it for her. Those were the days. Chasing love everywhere. Thinking her prince would someday come. Basing her whole life on romance while pretending not to.

Why was it that whenever she stopped chasing something and let go of her need to have it, it then just showed up. As if to say, *I'll visit you when you stop needing me.*

Did she need a relationship with Robert Chance? No. Did she want one? Madison hugged her tiger and shrugged. She looked him in the eyes and said, "I don't know. You tell me."

The white tiger said nothing.

46

Glen Gibbon was signing his lease agreements in the lobby of a tall apartment building in Denver. The building had a sign on the top floor outside that said, "Ballpark Lofts" because it was across the street from Coors Field and some of the units had a view of the baseball field where the Colorado Rockies played.

Gibbon didn't care about baseball. The woman who kept handing him his paperwork across the old oaken desk one sheet at a time for signatures looked to be in her mid-fifties. She had a purple and green flowered dress on and wore reading glasses with a sequined cord that went back behind her poofed up hair.

Gibbon thought she looked like Sitting Bull.

"So, Mr. Young, what kind of work do you do?" she said.

Gibbon looked at her in confusion. *Mr. Young?* And then it hit him that she was talking to Brock Young, not Glen Gibbon.

He smiled.

He liked having a new name.

He felt like he was in a spy movie. He wished Susan was here to see him pull this off. She would see that he wasn't such a simpleton after all. He always had an embarrassed feeling that his grammar was bad... or that he was misusing words around Susan. It made him hate his parents all the more for not bringing him up right. Worse: for not even *knowing* that they had not brought him up right. Hill apes. Frontier people when there was no frontier. Mouth breathers. Country folk living in the city.

He remembered his father singing his favorite song, *hey I said hello country bumpkin, how's the frost out on the pumpkin?*

Susan had been furious about the email he sent that was supposed to be from Tom. He'd never known her to be that angry. And for what? Just because he said "for you and I" instead of "for you and me"? How was that even wrong? Wasn't it *always* more educated to say "you and I"?

He'd sent the email just like he was told to from Tom's computer. So it wasn't perfect!

"You've only stirred up a sleeping, rabid dog!" she had shouted at him. Gibbon knew she meant Robert Chance. Why did he have to be an ex-cop? Why couldn't he just be one of those... what was he? ... secular spiritual advisors. Then he would have probably bought into the whole package.

No matter.

It was now going according to plan. Gibbon was executing masterfully. He was Brock Young now. No more ties to his parents. Goodbye country bumpkins! No more frost upon this pumpkin. No more ties to his difficult son or his redheaded mother.

He would just wait in Denver for Susan. It was going to be good now. She was not going to tease Brock Young the way she teased Gibbon. She was not going to just flirt with Brock Young to turn him on and get him to do things.

Brock Young would not allow that.

Brock Young would not be messed with.

47

Nikki and her brother, Chance, were having breakfast at her house. She'd made her special avocado and turkey sausage omelets, and Chance was enjoying the food, drinking his second cup of coffee and reading through her three new poems.

"You don't have to come to my book signing Sunday," said Nikki. "I'm only going to read those three poems and answer some questions. And I know you have your friend's church service."

"I'll be there," said Chance. "I admire your writing. And I love the way you answer questions. Especially the ones about why poetry doesn't sell like vampire novels."

"Poetry sells more than people realize," said Nikki. "And if it weren't for the vampire books there wouldn't be bookstores for me to read in."

"Is Janet coming?" Chance said. Janet had been Nikki's partner for twelve years.

"She's in New York," said Nikki. "She's a judge at the Tribeca Film Festival there."

"You and Janet amaze me. You're so different and yet so close."

"We like those differences."

Chance set his plate aside and held his coffee cup with two hands as if lost in thought.

"What is it?" said Nikki.

"What is what?"

"Well, you came all the way here to tell me that Janet and I amazed you? What are you thinking about?"

"Oh, I don't know for sure."

Nikki grinned, "Something to do with two people being together who have differences but still make it work. That would be my guess. If I *had to* guess what you were thinking about."

"You guess pretty well. Why don't you just do my work?"

"Coaching?"

"Investigation. Because you can read minds it seems and that would save a lot of time for an investigator."

"Who is she?"

"Who is who?"

"Her name, please."

"Madison."

"Like James Madison?"

"Madison is a woman's name, Nik, and a pretty cool one, at that."

"What does she do?"

"She's an internet marketing consultant and she's now doing some investigation work."

"And you have begun to care about her on more than a professional level."

"Do I even need to speak? Why don't you just tell me what my life is all about?"

Nikki laughed and stood up to feed her African Grey Parrot that had begun to repeat the word *Janet!* in the cage next to the kitchen window.

"Differences are the best things," said Nikki. "Without them you have boredom. Bring her to my reading. I'll tell you if she's right for you."

"By the way she responds to your poems?"

"No. By the way you look at her when she's listening to me."

"I wish all women were like you."

"You wouldn't have any girlfriends if they were."

"Oh, well, there's that, too. You know something, she once asked me what kind of flower I thought she was."

"You said she was a flower?"

"No, I was talking about personal growth... the stages we have to pass through... like a flower."

"You seem somewhat enchanted, Robert. What flower did you think of?"

"I couldn't think. She's kind of dazzling sometimes and it stops the thinking process."

"That sounds like Amaryllis. The flower she might be."

"Okay... I like those."

"Well, then you can tell her that next time she asks you what flower she reminds you of. The botanic name Amaryllis is taken from a shepherdess in Virgil's pastoral poems. The name is from a Greek word that means to sparkle."

"Perfect. Perfect for her. I'll want to remember that. Sometimes I wish I were the poet and you were the cop."

Chance gave his sister a goodbye hug. It's not a boring world, he thought. A world that can have both poetry and crime in it.

 **48**

Madison woke up to a clock radio that played her Gould CD of Bach's Goldberg Variations. Could a piano player play those pieces without caffeine? These were the kinds of things she wondered about in the morning.

She splashed cold water on her face and put on a tattered pink robe. It was kind of a raggedy robe and she knew it. But she also loved it because her father had given it to her long ago.

She made green tea and put two whole grain frozen blueberry waffles in the toaster. She'd have those with raw organic honey while going over her application forms to the online university's fast-track police science course.

The sooner she was a certified and licensed investigator the happier she would be.

She brought her tea into her office and logged onto her computer. She decided to look into Gibbon for a while. Glen Gibbon's applications for forms of I.D. now had her looking in other areas. Was he flying somewhere soon? She was frustrated everywhere she looked until she just Googled his name to see if there was anything there.

Sometimes the most obvious ideas are overlooked. All his recent real estate dealings turned up and so did an *L.A. Times* online news item.

"Real Estate Broker Reported Missing" said the headline. She read further. Gibbon had been reported missing by his office receptionist and secretary. The article noted that Gibbon's son

Garon was in custody, held on suspicion of starting the arson fire in Laurel Canyon.

She grabbed her phone and called Chance, but it went straight to voice mail. She'd see him at ten. Things were moving faster than she wanted them to.

49

Chance met Madison at his front door. They both watched an orange and white tabby cat run across his front yard and crawl under Madison's green Volvo.

Madison said, "Is that cat yours?"

"I was going to ask you the same thing. It's under your car. No. No cats for me. Angie would never adjust."

"It's a Morris cat," said Madison. "I knew an ad agency account exec once, a competitor of mine, his name was Morris and he called himself Morris the Cat."

"Sounds classy."

"He used to say, 'Hi I'm Morris the Cat and I can make your business meow.'"

"I'm glad you changed fields. You'll meet less creepy people in the world of crime."

Chance called into the house, "It's not her cat, Angie."

Angie the retriever heard her name and came to the front door, tail thumping against the screen. They stepped in and Madison began massaging the top of Angie's head.

"Mind if we sit down today in the kitchen?" Chance said. "I have menudo in the crock pot and the coffee, tea, and bagels are all there."

"Menudo? How can you stand menudo? Isn't it basically tripe?"

"But why think of it that way? It's a true southwestern delight and a perfect cure for a hangover."

"Are you hung over?"

"Yes. But not from liquor. Although I did have one bourbon with Sue Dumar, I don't think that's what causing the hangover."

"What are you hung over from?"

"The meeting itself. It went nowhere and yet everywhere. There's just no more doubt for me that she's in this thing neck deep. She has none of the normal grieving widow human response anymore. Maybe she never did."

"And Gibbon's secretary reported him missing, according to the *LA Times* internet edition."

"How did *that* happen? What an idiot. He leaves town and doesn't tell anyone anything. Just doesn't show up for work? Every time I think this thing is diabolically clever someone does something so stupid I don't know what to think anymore."

"Could there be foul play? Could someone have taken him out or away?"

"I don't think so. I'm guessing not... but I don't know."

"Did he leave to go spend his share of the insurance money?"

"Not for the fire. That insurance payout is just not going to happen. But Tom's life insurance should have paid out."

"Well, I found out that Tom took that out five years ago and his company, Brigadier Life, has a thirteen-month waiting period for suicide," Madison said. "It was a two million dollar policy."

"You do good work. It's a shame you're not working for Mossi right now or he'd open the case up as possible homicide and Brigadier would have withheld its payout for as long as Susan was a person of interest."

"Why don't we just go to Mossi with everything we've got so far? He'd open it if he knew everything we knew. He'd have to eat crow, but he could claim new developments, etc."

"Eat crow is right. Like no real investigation occurred, no decent police work."

"Can we get him to do it?"

"The question is, do we want to?"

"What do you mean?"

"What are we trying to achieve? What's our ideal scene?"

"Ideal scene? This sounds like coaching."

"Well, only because coaching, when it's done right, is about finding the truth. And finding beauty. Truth *and* beauty. They're always the same thing."

"I don't see that at all, and you know what? How about we have an agreement where I can just snap my fingers and bring you back to Earth? Like a hypnotist. Snap my fingers and your Zen thing goes away and you talk to me like a normal person."

Chance was smiling as he got up to answer the shrieking tea kettle. He found a cup for Madison and a tray for the cream and sweeteners. He fumbled around with bringing them all out at once, and then just brought out the cup. He would make three trips instead of one. Four, if necessary. He wasn't used to serving tea. Going back to get the tea bags he said, "Chamomile, mint, or English Breakfast?"

"English Breakfast. I need to stay awake to keep following you. What is our ideal scene, as you put it?"

"To find truth and beauty — always the same thing — and get to the bottom of this whole thing so that no one escapes responsibility."

"Okay, but how does letting Mossi close the Tom Dumar case help us do that? How does seeing the fire as a separate arson case do that? What if they close that one, too, and Gibbon, Gibbon-the-father, and Susan Dumar, assuming she's involved, escape into the woodwork? How does that help us?"

"We watch them escape."

"And that's good?"

"Yes. We want them to escape, for now, so we can see what they do. We want the police out of this for now so we can do what we do better. Once Gibbon and Susan think their cases are closed, they will do more interesting things. They'll be less cautious. They'll become more observable."

"I am starting to see it. So it's almost better, for our purposes, that they got away with the first part of this."

"Yes."

"But Gibbon's gone already."

"Yes. That's fine. We will find him. *You* will find him."

"You have a lot of faith in me," said Madison.

"I do. I have faith. I have trust. And I have a question."

"I knew you would." Madison pulled her laptop out of her bag so she could answer whatever Chance asked about.

"My question is this," said Chance. "Will you go to a poetry reading with me Sunday?"

Madison looked up from her laptop and turned her head in a questioning angle. Chance thought she looked like Angie.

"My sister Nikki is reading," said Chance. "And she's pretty good."

"Of course, I'd love that. I've never met your sister."

Chance walked to a shelf by the windows where his unused cookbooks were lined up and he pulled Nikki's new book of poetry, *Everyone Travels by Sea*, from the shelf. He handed it to Madison. She looked at the front and back cover, and then looked up.

"Is this going to be a coaching session or investigative?" said Madison.

"Is what going to be?"

"Our going to the reading."

"Let's not label it for now."

"But for my journal, what should I say it is? A date?"

Chance laughed and poured himself another cup of coffee.

"I would not be the one to choose the words for your journal," he said.

"No, but my journal wants to know what words you might choose for yourself."

Chance thought about his answer. It reminded him of a time he was on patrol chasing a suspected drug dealer who was in a tiny Nissan pickup. The dealer took a side street and ended up in a cul-de-sac. Chance thought he had him trapped until the dealer drove his little truck across a lawn, through someone's back yard, through a flimsy fence and off to freedom. Chance hadn't felt it was appropriate to chase him through back yards in a police vehicle.

"It's hard to find words," Chance said, "for the experience of being with you."

Madison felt her face flush and had a hard time looking up to meet his eyes.

When she did she said, "My journal will accept that."

50

The poet Nikki Chance was introduced by an ebullient woman who couldn't get over how many people had crowded into her little bookstore to hear the reading. She went through all her thank yous and the plans for the cookies and the signing of Nikki's book later, and began reading the names of the authors coming to do readings the next three months.

Madison and Chance were in the third row and Madison leaned over to whisper to him.

"You still haven't told me about the church service this morning."

"Uneventful," said Chance. "Very solemn, surprisingly sparse. No friends or family spoke. Susan was there. Dressed in black. No surprises."

"Really."

"Except maybe one."

"What was that?"

"Mossi. Detective Mossi, LAPD, was there. Stood out at the edge."

"How interesting."

The room was filled with the noise of clapping and some whooping.

Nikki walked to the front of the room smiling. Her silver blonde hair was short but stylishly spiked. She wore copper and turquoise hooped earrings. Her faded blue denim shirt was neatly pressed with gold wing patterns sewn above the pockets. She wore loose-fitting white jeans and tan moccasins with red and blue beads.

Chance thought she had moccasins like that when she was a little girl. Nikki looked radiant to him, her green eyes lit up and that constant peaceful almost Mona Lisa smile. It was as if all of life to Nik was just one simple blessing after another. Where did she get that? Was it in the seminary studying her theology? No, it went back even further. She was the happiest little girl he'd ever known.

She stepped up to the small podium and microphone and Chance caught a glimpse of Madison watching and listening. Nikki said, "This one began as a song and became a poem and went back to being a song again. I almost didn't include it because of that, but it became the one people seemed to like the most."

No more grapevines
or dust bowls
or pastures of wrath.
No more hard traveled dreams,
no more blistering path

Chance watched the crowd in the bookstore listen as the verses continued. It was quite a crowd… everyone there from little old ladies to power lesbians wearing canine collars and tattoos. Men, too, smiling with their eyes as Nikki read. Maybe poetry was making a comeback. Maybe Nik would usher in a whole new appreciation for the beauty of the word. Chance thought of Charles Mingus. He said creativity was awesomely simple. Nikki read on to the song's final words:

No more tracks laid at midnight
or boyfriends for me.
Now thank God everyone
travels by sea.

She wasn't afraid to rhyme. Chance liked that. Most contemporary poetry did not rhyme. But Chance liked the constraint. He thought constraints made people rise up, get more inspired, not less.

The same with his own life. He had lifted too many of the constraints when he went into coaching. His workouts with his trainer Wu Li had become too sporadic. His reading had drifted down into magazines and blogs.

But this investigation somehow was returning invigorating constraints to his life. Driving him beyond where coaching had taken him. The obstacles were refreshing. Problems always brought out the best in him... the adventurer within, the peaceful warrior that always wanted to be in action. He'd left the police department for coaching because he wanted more freedom. But the constraints and restrictions of crime and the law had value too. And right now they were allowing him to rise up and become inspired.

It was like having to deal with meter and rhyme.

Nikki's line, "everyone travels by sea," seemed to cause her throat to catch, and Chance could see that she had tears in her eyes; and when the room erupted in applause, he saw that Madison was shaking her head while she was clapping.

Madison looked over at Chance. Chance lifted his eyebrows and shoulders in a well-what-do-you-think? kind of gesture and Madison said, "She is your sister. She is definitely your sister."

Chance decided to take that as a compliment, and as Nikki began reading another poem he felt his cell phone vibrate in his pocket. *I shouldn't have brought it in here.* But he'd also told Mossi where he'd be today and to call if something big came up.

Chance whispered in Madison's ear and weaved his way through the crowd listening to Nikki toward the back of the bookstore. He found an emergency exit and examined the door to see that it wouldn't set off some kind of alarm. It didn't look like it would, so he slipped outside to the alley behind the store.

He saw that his "missed call" was Mossi so he punched Mossi's number and waited.

"Mossi," said Mossi.

"Chance."

"Your girl Susan Dumar didn't go back to her sister's house directly after the service."

"Where did she go?"

"She pulled into a Wal-Mart parking lot and sat there for ten minutes and then a mystery man got into her car. She talked to that someone for about an hour. Then she tore out of there like lightning."

"Back to her sister's?"

"Yup."

"Who was she talking to in the lot?"

"Couldn't tell."

"What did he look like?"

"Couldn't tell."

"Why not?"

"His head was wrapped in bandages."

"Bandages?"

"Like he'd been in a fire or something."

"His whole head?"

"Looked like it."

"Where did *he* go?"

"Lost him."

"How?"

"He was on foot. I sent my partner after him while I tailed Mrs. Dumar. The phantom of the opera walked into Wal-Mart and we never saw him again."

"That's it?"

"Come see me tomorrow?"

"I'll call you."

Chance threaded his way through the crowd back to his seat next to Madison. Her expression wanted answers but he put a finger to his lips and smiled as if everything in life was a simple pleasure.

They both turned to listen to the end of Nikki's reading.

51

Gibbon stared out of his window and looked down at Coors Field. People were lining up for tickets to the baseball game, and he wondered what going to a game would be like if he didn't know anything about baseball.

He'd just end up hating the game and the people who yelled about it.

All that false trumped-up loyalty. Loyalty to what? Some desperate clinging to the team as an extension of themselves? No wonder people got so upset when their team lost. *If the team is me, I'm a loser.*

Those people are losers, thought Gibbon, even when they think they're winning.

He didn't need this new line of thought. Forget baseball. The hatred he already felt was quite enough. He needed a way to relieve it until life played itself out and she would come be with him.

What would *her* new name be? Would she want to become Mrs. Brock Young? What was it she told him? *I will make you feel pleasure you've never felt?* He went to the dresser in his bedroom to get his wallet where he kept the little piece of paper with those words written on it.

Pathetic.

That he actually wrote that down.

Most women, if they found out you were following them, would turn you in to the police. Gibbon preferred the word "following" although *she* had called it stalking. She said she *would* have turned him in if she hadn't found him so interesting. Could he trust that? And if she found him so attractive, why did it never go anywhere? He'd tried to hold her a few times and she always said, "Not yet."

Not yet.

Only after it's over.

"Well, it's *over*," Gibbon said aloud as he smacked his fat wallet back on the dresser without reading the folded paper in it.

He looked around his bedroom. Ballpark loft. Would she sleep with him here? He felt a funny feeling in the base of his throat when he thought about that. A tingle. Same feeling he had when he watched his father kill rabbits in the back yard.

Like he wanted to growl like a werewolf.

Better fix this place up a little, he thought. The bed would need sheets. For her. He himself didn't care. He could sleep on a bare mattress in his clothes. Like he did when he was a little boy. He was beyond caring. But her? She had class. She was the high life. Made fun of his grammar. Knew how to dress. Always.

His only question: does she know how to undress?

Gibbon felt the tingle come up again. Just at the base of the throat. Like he wanted to kill a rabbit.

And not later, but right away.

52

Carrie Makem said she'd meet her friends at the end of the pier in Santa Monica for their Friday ritual. Her post on the internet said, "I'm skipping fifth hour because we have a sub and he'll be a retard who won't know how to report it so I'll get there early. But I've got my *Twilight* so I'll be in vampire heaven with Edward no matter how long you guys take to get there. This is my third time with *Twilight*."

Madison sat back from her computer and wondered if Carrie had a car. Not at fifteen. But public transportation in Santa Monica was better than anywhere in the LA area, so Carrie would be able to hop on the Big Blue Bus Line and find her freedom very quickly.

●　●　●

Madison parked her car far up the hill from the pier. She had her walking shoes on and a grey tank top and blue silk track shorts. She didn't know exactly what she was doing, but if nothing came to nothing she at least wanted to get some good exercise doing it.

Her hair was pulled back by an Eminem headband she'd gotten from her niece Hayley for Christmas. What would Carrie Makem think of her? She'll *probably think I'm a mom.*

But a young mom.

Madison got out of her car with her mind on babies. Where did that train of thought come from?

You're getting your life together finally, and you start fantasizing babies? Do you sabotage yourself just for fun? But how could a baby be a form of sabotage? Without babies, no human race. That feels like the opposite of sabotage.

Madison reached into her backpack and pulled out a plastic bottle of water and took a deep drink.

Pull yourself together.

You don't even have a husband.

The babies wouldn't have a father.

She laughed. She shook her hair and splashed some water on her face from the bottle And felt better. It was nice not to have make-up on. I'll look younger to Carrie without it. She picked up her walking pace into a leisurely jog. She could see the Ferris wheel at the pier a mile ahead. She looked forward to being near the ocean.

Madison reached Ocean Avenue, waited at the light, and crossed over to the pier. She always had mixed feelings about the pier. It was crowded, tacky and touristy, yet there was something innocently friendly about it. There was also the thrill of walking two thousand feet over the Pacific on a hundred-year-old wood piling. She loved walking on the pier and breathing in the smell of fish and wood.

She liked knowing that the Ferris wheel was the first solar powered wheel in the world. Every time she saw it go around she realized that it was spinning from the sun. She had great memories, too, of her first Ferris wheel ride as a little girl seeing out across the Pacific from the top, imagining that she was queen of an ocean world.

As she walked down the pier to the very end where Carrie said she would be, she observed all the amazing variations of human enterprise. Shops, kiosks, and even a panhandler. She remembered that Paul Newman's character in *The Sting* worked here on this pier, running his charming scams.

Was this a sting operation that Madison was running? Nothing *that* convoluted, she hoped. Chance always said to keep it simple and so she would. She wanted to talk to Carrie about Glen Gibbon, now listed as a missing person.

This case keeps getting harder and harder for that Detective Mossi to close. Madison shook her head as she walked past the shops and stalls selling chains and bracelets. Did she look ridiculous at her age wearing an Eminem headband? She didn't care.

Would Paul Newman care?

She arrived at the end of the pier where a young tattooed woman in a print dress was playing guitar and singing, "I tried to be chill but you're so hot that I melted…" and saw an old man with a fishing pole leaning over the rail accompanied by a boy who looked to be his grandson with a pole of his own. The grandson was fidgety and the old man was silent and still. Fishing can be hard for the young at first. Especially here. What could really be caught here? Yet their two coffee cans filled with water seemed to have little fish in them. Maybe it was bait?

Madison took her backpack off and sat down. She checked her cell phone for messages and was a little disappointed that there weren't any. But Chance wasn't a real cell phone kind of guy. He kept things pretty basic on that score.

After no more than twenty minutes of relaxing and watching the old man and his grandson fish, she saw Carrie Makem. She was walking very quickly toward the pier's end with a book in one hand and a canvas bag over her shoulder. She looked around and found a place to sit near the fisherman. Her bright red hair was spiked and looked almost comical in the sun. Her face was freckled and a little flushed from the ocean breezes and she looked happy.

Once she was seated and had looked out over the ocean for a while, she settled into her book. The book was a huge glossy black paperback with two pale female hands on the cover cradling a bright red apple. The title *Twilight* reminded Madison of a different twilight… the twilight film series she used to attend on this pier when she was in college. Should she disturb this girl?

Carrie kept looking up from her book and checking her phone. She held her phone up toward the old man and his grandson and took a picture. Then she texted something and seemed to be smiling at the message.

Madison decided to approach her.

"Excuse me, but are you Carrie Makem?" she said with a friendly smile as if she was surprised to see her here. Carrie Makem was not so friendly. She looked around like there might be more Madison Kerrs coming to confront her. When you skip school, no matter how much of a retard your substitute is, you don't feel totally safe talking to adults.

"Do I know you?" said Carrie.

Madison was relieved. At least that question confirmed that this was Carrie. Where to take it from here? Madison wished she had thought this through a little bit more ahead of time. But how do you rehearse a conversation with a teenager?

You're lucky if they even talk to you.

"My name is Madison and I recognized your face from the internet. I'm helping some people try to find your father."

"I don't have a father."

Carrie looked around again to see if there were more grown-ups like this one coming. Sometimes they traveled in groups like the hyenas she saw on the Discovery Channel.

"What do you mean find him?" Carrie finally said. "Is he lost? That would actually be a good thing. I don't know anyone who would want to find him except… are you police?"

"No, no!" Madison said. "Can I sit down?"

Carrie said nothing and just stared at Madison. Madison sat down.

"I'm not even a private investigator but I'm going to take some courses soon. Right now I'm just helping someone I know. And I'm interested in finding your father."

"I don't know why you're talking to me," Carrie said. "He was always creepy around me and my mom made him stay way from both of us."

Madison looked at Carrie and looked out at the ocean. She pulled the band off of her head and shook her hair loose.

"That's fairly cool," said Carrie. "Eminem."

"You like him?"

"He's old but he's still cool."

"I know he's old. That's why I like him," said Madison. "That you can be that old and still do hip hop... that inspires me."

"Are you as old as him?"

"Oh no, I'm not *that* old. Do I look that old to you?"

Carrie shrugged and looked away. She looked back at Madison and said, "What do you want to know about my father?"

"I don't know,"said Madison. "I don't know what I want to know."

Carrie shook her head, "You sound like me. They ask me questions in school and I always say *I don't know.* I don't *know* what I want. I don't know *anything* about what I want to study or learn or even know."

"Welcome to the club."

"There's a club for that?"

"I don't know that either."

Carrie smiled. She looked like she was trying to decide whether to talk anymore.

Madison said, "I think it's good that you don't know things. And I'm happy just to know that you don't know."

"You are weird," said Carrie with a start of a smile.

Madison breathed deeply and looked at the water. There were bobbing ripples on the blue-green surface. The rhythmic whooshing wave sounds temporarily relaxed her. Something bobbed up; was it a shark? Maybe just a dolphin.

Carrie said, "My stepfather disappeared, too. And my mother thinks my father made that happen. That's all I know. And she won't ever let me talk about it."

Madison reached out and grabbed Carrie's hand. Something told her it was time to leave. She stood up. She picked her Eminem band up from the ground.

"Thank you, Carrie," she said.

"For what? What are you going to do?"

"I don't know."

Carrie stared at her. Madison gave Carrie her Eminem headband.

"Would you like this?"

Carrie said nothing, but took the headband and put it in her sack.

She looked back up at Madison, squinting in the sun. "Thank you," she said and Madison looked at her one last time before turning to walk the pier. She thought about what Carrie had said.

And my mother thinks my father made that happen.

She stopped after walking a few yards. She went back to where Carrie sat, now texting someone on her phone. Madison wrote her name and phone number on an empty page in her small notebook and tore it out and handed it to Carrie. Carrie took it, looked at it and put it in her sack. Madison smiled and pantomimed, "call me," and turned and walked slowly down the pier.

53

Madison and Chance met in the lobby of the Getty Research Library in Brentwood. Chance had worked all morning with a coaching client in Brentwood and asked Madison to meet him in the lobby of the library.

"Ever been here before?" said Chance.

"Yes, in college. I did part of a research paper here on architecture."

"I got us a study room in the basement. Probably as private a public place as you'll find in all of LA."

They took an elevator down and walked down a long dimly lit hall to a room with a small window in the door. Chance pulled out a business card from his back pocket, read some writing on the back of it, and punched a code in the box by the door handle. He opened the door and gestured for Madison to enter. There was a rectangular wooden table and four wooden chairs, two on each side. An old-fashioned blackboard was on one wall with a tray of thick cylinders of white chalk. Chance and Madison sat down, Chance opening a tattered spiral notebook and Madison pulling a laptop from her backpack.

"So Detective Mossi saw Susan Dumar talking to a man with bandages on his head," said Madison, her fingers making clicking sounds across the keyboard of her laptop. "A lot of bandages? So much so that he couldn't make an ID?"

"You've got the lingo down now, don't you? Yes, the head was almost totally bandaged so Mossi went back to check with the fire department and the hospital on injuries in that fire."

"I thought there were no serious injuries. Except for Susan's fish."

"We all thought that, which is why Mossi is going back to check again. But there's something about Wal-Mart that's troubling me."

"Certainly not their prices."

"No, it's something Tom Dumar said in a coaching session once long ago about his wife finding a younger lover. He was very suspicious. And I could swear that he said some handsome young guy who was a dock manager at Wal-Mart had been paying Susan a lot of attention."

"Maybe Mossi will find out more about him," said Madison. "But I thought you wanted Mossi to wrap this up so our suspects would feel free to play their next hand."

"I did, but I don't always get what I want."

"That's hard to believe."

"What about your meeting with Gibbon's daughter? What happened with that?"

"I met her, but I kind of chickened out," said Madison. "I backed off. All of a sudden I wasn't an investigator any more. I just felt for her. I just walked away."

"But she said something?"

"She said her mother has kept Gibbon away. She said she thought Gibbon made her stepfather go away. Carrie said he was so creepy her mom had to keep him away."

"Do the custody courts act on reports of people being creepy? Don't you have to have something more substantial than that? If that was all you needed no one would be allowed to see anybody anymore."

Madison nodded and stood up to stretch. She walked to the blackboard and picked up a stick of white chalk.

"I didn't know they still had these," she said. "You see them in all the old movies. Real blackboards." She drew a circle and the chalk broke and half the stick fell to the floor. She bent down to pick it up. "Whiteboards with dry erase markers are more practical," she said.

But Chance was only half listening to her. He, too, drew a circle on a page on his notebook and then another circle inside that one.

"If Gibbon shot Tom and made it look like a suicide," said Chance, "why would he allow himself to be reported missing? Why wouldn't he buy himself more time? Like maybe let his administrative assistant go or just make it look to her like he was leaving town on a business trip?"

"Because he's not very smart? Because he's not really a criminal?"

"That would fit, him not really being a criminal, if Tom wasn't killed by him. But aren't we operating on a pretty good deduction that Gibbon did this?"

"What if Tom was induced into killing himself? Talked into it? Hypnotized, or something like that?"

"Not likely."

"Do you know anything about hypnotism?"

"I know a little, and I have a friend, who's also my trainer, who has been into hypnosis for years. Maybe I'll ask him tonight."

"A trainer? What kind?"

"His name is Wu Li. He does physical workouts, a few martial arts techniques, that kind of thing."

"And hypnosis, too?"

"He knows a lot of strange and wonderful tricks. He's Chinese, and I've been working with him for ten years."

"Is he where you get your weird Zen stuff?"

Chance laughed. "I'm sure I get some of it from Wu Li. But from everything I know about hypnosis, you can't really make people do something they don't really want to do."

"So let's just assume Gibbon did something very bad to Tom or else why would he leave town leaving his son behind and his assistant so freaked out she reports him as a missing person?"

This time Chance walked up to the blackboard. He drew a rough map of California and arrows pointing in various directions from LA. He walked back to the table and grabbed his water bottle and took a drink. He was stuck, but he enjoyed being with Madison.

Chance said, "It's a good assumption that Gibbon did something bad to Tom."

"What would we do next, then? If that was true?"

"I would introduce myself to Gibbon's alias Brock Young and employ some advanced interrogation techniques."

"You would go look for Gibbon?"

"Yes. I think moving quickly now makes sense. Remember that Mossi said that Susan met with a guy in a car with a bandage wrapped around his head. That's not normal behavior on a funeral day. He said they talked for an hour. So I would say it's time for me to pick up the pace."

"Can I go look for him with you?"

"No."

Madison realized that pouting right now would not be very professional. She began typing on her keyboard to lift herself out of her emotions and back into her logical mind. "Will you be safe doing some kind of manhunt?" she said, but wished she hadn't. It was not an investigator's question.

"Maybe not," said Chance. "But if I wanted to be safe I'd have left this whole case alone. I would have let the justice system and the powers that be take their own course."

"But they weren't taking much of a course. It was just an open-and-shut suicide. If you hadn't objected to the scenario they were buying, there probably wouldn't have even been a fire."

"See what I've done? So I think I've forfeited my right to be safe, but how safe is anyone, really?"

Madison shook her head.

Chance said, "Do you think Gibbon will contact his daughter or his son?"

"I gave Carrie my number. I don't know exactly why. Who knows what could happen? And I'm sure Brock Young, as he calls himself, has a new cell that no one can track yet."

Chance's cell phone vibrated and he pulled it from his pocket and looked at the small screen that said, "Mossi."

"It's him, our favorite detective," said Chance. "Boy, he's really into this thing now. We may have to work with him after all."

Madison shrugged and pointed to Chance's still-vibrating phone.

Chance opened his phone, stood up and answered it. He pushed the little panel that changed it to "speaker" mode so Madison would hear the detective.

"Chance, I got an order to track Susan Dumar's land line phone calls from a very unhappy judge who couldn't find cause."

"How did you do that?"

"Some day I'll teach you how a real detective gets things done," said Mossi. "And she took three calls from a pay phone in Denver. Do you know what that's all about?"

"I wouldn't know," said Chance. "Where was the pay phone?"

"Coors Field. The ballpark. They have phones next to the ticket window outside the stadium."

"Wow. That's a head-scratcher," said Chance, giving an innocent look to Madison who was shaking her head. Chance chalked a huge "DENVER" on the blackboard.

Mossi said, "Well, since you're freelancing this thing and since you're Captain America and a psychic to boot, I thought you could tell me what that might be."

"No, but I'll look into it. Are you opening this whole case back up, Detective? The suicide and the whole thing?"

"Hell, no! I just don't want another Covington girl case... the missing girl you found to make us look bad. I know how you work. You leave the department and then you come back and show the department that they don't have anybody as good as you."

"That never happened, Sergeant Mossi. I was just doing a job."

"Okay. But keep me included in this thing. I'm not fighting you anymore on this one. I brought you in to help with interrogation. You don't need to humiliate me."

"That won't happen. I do have one question though."

"What."

"Why, if you're not opening Tom Dumar's suicide, were you at his funeral and tailing his wife?"

"Arson," said Mossi. "Remember? That's our case, and their house was the target."

"Okay," said Chance. "Keep *me* in the loop on that case, will you?"

"Sure will," said Mossi and he was gone.

Madison let a moment go by and then said to Chance, "Don't men say goodbye?"

"What do you mean?"

"I mean, on cell phones, do men just close the phone when they're finished talking without saying good bye? Neither you nor Mossi said good bye to each other. It just seems rude."

"It's not rude."

"What is it?"

"Time management."

"Oh, my. How unsentimental. Maybe you can get Michael Jackson's 'Never Can Say Goodbye' as your ringtone. Give your persona a little artistic touch."

"Would you know how to do that?"

"Sure."

"You're on. I love that song."

54

Chance showed up at Wu Li's gym wearing faded jeans cutoffs and a black tee shirt with the sleeves torn off.

He wished he wasn't there.

Wu Li greeted him at the door and shook his hand and bowed to him. "Ready for a great session?" he said.

The gym was in the basement of a former YMCA building that had been converted into a soup kitchen. There weren't any windows and thick gymnastic pads covered the floor. Chance removed his shoes and said, "Today I am almost completely out of energy, but I know this is where I need to be."

Wu Li smiled and said, "I am happy, Robert. Out of energy is a good place to be to start a workout."

"Why is that? I'm sure you've told me before."

"Because it's what you do when you don't want to do it that matters most in your growth. Doing only what you want stops growth. Pushing through is the skill we're developing."

"Pushing through."

"Yes. Not always easy for Americans to understand."

Wu Li had lectured Chance many times about how his Chinese people were in the process of taking over the world.

"You Americans are too soft now," he would say. "You have lost the work ethic. We Chinese are ready to take our turn."

"Then why are you here in America?" Chance would say. "Why are you in California? Why did Bruce Lee come here? Why does Jet Li make movies here if China is so superior?"

Wu Li would just smile. He had posters of Bruce Lee and Jet Li in his gym. "These are my favorite Americans," he would say of them. "They are just partly Chinese, like me. But their best part is Chinese."

Chance owed his entire sense of himself physically to Wu Li's sessions. When he met Wu Li he had a lot of physical fears. Wearing a firearm helped with that, or so he thought. But he found that it only covered his physical fears up.

Wu Li said he would take away those fears altogether.

"So you believe in the whole mind-body connection," Chance had said when he was introduced to Wu Li by a fellow cop. Chance thought he believed in mind-body, too, although his many psychotherapy sessions and spiritual meditation retreats hadn't taken his physical fears away. They just helped him accept them and live a happier life, anyway.

But Wu Li did *not* believe in mind-body, which initially confused Chance until he understood.

Wu Li even looked a lot like Bruce Lee as he stood in front of Chance that first day with black basketball trunks and a white v-neck tee shirt. "It's body-mind with me," said Wu Li. "Not mind-body. It's body-mind."

Chance would soon begin to learn what Wu Li meant. You transform the body and the mind follows. Wu Li said that was almost correct, but not quite there.

"What is it, then?" Chance had said.

"Body-mind means the body does not *lead* the mind, but the body *is* the mind. You westerners are obsessed with the mind. That's why you stay stuck there. Never *do* anything remarkable. Just *think* remarkable things."

Chance was willing to go along with anything Wu Li believed because his workouts gave him a different kind of strength than he ever had before.

On this weary night tonight Chance was doing his twentieth push-up when Wu Li kneeled down next to him and began placing pressure with his open palm between Chance's shoulder blades.

"What is this you're doing?" Chance said as the push-ups got harder each time Wu Li pressed down.

"Surprising your muscles," said Wu Li. "They were too bored."

"How can a muscle that's pushing up a couple hundred pounds be bored?"

"Muscles relax into robotic motion and do not grow... like people do not grow... think the same thoughts, do the same things all day, don't grow."

"I'm thinking new thoughts now," said Chance, straining with all his might against Wu Li's palm pressure to finish his set of 30. 23. 24. 25. "I'm going to Denver tomorrow to chase down a lead."

26. 27. 28. And the pressure on his back was becoming ridiculous. Wu Li was pressing down harder with every push upward.

"Push through!" Wu Li shouted. "Push *through* me. Don't let me defeat you. Surprise me. Surprise yourself. Stop being you! Just be the pushing. Unstoppable! Unstoppable!"

Chance couldn't think any more. All he could do was push into the pain in the back of his arms, yelling, "Too much pain!" and wishing he hadn't. 29! 29 was taking forever but there, I'm all the way up. Here comes 30. *Oh no, he's got both hands on my back now. Is he sitting on me?*

"*Cause* the pain," whispered Wu Li in Chance's ear. "*Cause* the pain. Don't fight it; cause it. Make the pain come *from you,* not me. Make pain and push."

Chance pushed with all his might causing waves of pain and a dizzy feeling behind his eyes. More pain. And pale blue lights, blue ovals of light inside his closed eyes as Wu Li jumped off and 30 was finished. Thirty push-ups. Exactly what he set out to do. And these were deep, full pushups, not the mini-pushups he saw most men do. These were Wu Li pushups, with the chest touching the floor each time.

Chance rolled over on his back and looked up through his burning eyes at Wu Li who was smiling broadly. Wu Li went to a cabinet by the wall and pulled out a white towel and tossed it to Chance.

"What's this about chasing a lead in Denver?" Wu Li said. "I thought you weren't a cop anymore, or is this a business lead?"

"I'm trying to find out who killed my friend. In fact, I'll probably be going to Denver to talk to the person who killed my friend."

"Sounds like a Chinese martial arts movie. Why not take Wu Li with you?"

"No, no. That's why I come here. I want you to put whatever Wu Li is into *me* so I don't have to take you with me. And I don't like the look on your face. The minute I said someone killed my friend you lit up. What's that all about? Don't the Chinese have any compassion?"

"Chinese move on," said Wu Li. "There is no death of friend, just moving on."

"And revenge?"

"A work of art," said Wu Li, "when it's done right."

Chance laughed. Wu Li went to the water cooler and drew a cup of water for Chance, and then for himself.

"So my going to Denver is like a martial arts movie to you."

"Remember *Enter the Dragon*?" said Wu Li. "If you are going to Denver to find the killer of your friend, you can be like Bruce Lee in that movie and you'll be okay. Do not be like an American. No Rambo or Bruce Willis. You will get hurt or worse. You will embarrass yourself."

"God forbid."

"Or even worse than that, Robert, you will get killed and that will embarrass Wu Li. You are a student of Wu Li."

"How could I forget?" said Chance, rotating his arms slowly to see if the burning feeling in his triceps might subside.

"So, what then?" said Chance.

"What?"

"What did Bruce Lee say or do in *Enter the Dragon* that I want to remember? And I do own that movie, so I can watch it tonight to check your accuracy if I have to."

"You will want to." Wu Li pulled a three-legged stool from the corner and sat to face Chance. "Watch how Bruce Lee says 'When the opponent expands, I contract. When he contracts, I expand. And when there is an opportunity, I do not hit.'"

"You do *not* hit?"

"And when there is an opportunity, I do not hit. It hits all by itself."

Chance took a long drink of water. He said, slowly, "It hits all by itself."

"Yes. It does."

"What is *it*?" said Chance. "What is it that does that... that hits all by itself."

"What is it that pushed through when it was too hard to do?" said Wu Li. "What is it that has you wanting to make things right with your friend?"

"Make them clear."

"Clear them up?" said Wu Li.

Chance knew he'd never find words for it because in Wu Li's world it starts with the wordless body anyway. There wasn't a mind; there was a body-mind and right now Chance's was hurting. But there was also that warm, quiet feeling he got every time he met with Wu Li. The feeling that there was more to him than when he arrived.

Wu Li and Chance bowed and hugged and Wu Li turned his attention to two new students who were warming up in the far corner of the gym by lying on their backs and doing bicycling motions with their legs.

"Lance Armstrong!" shouted Wu Li. "Lance Armstrong is honorary Chinaman to Wu Li!"

Chance walked to the wall and looked at the "Wu Li 20" list of exercises he would put himself through before leaving, always with Wu Li's watchful observation from whatever corner of the gym he was in.

When he was finished he opened the door and climbed the stairs into the soup kitchen's waiting room and then out to the refreshingly brisk cool night air. He stretched his arms up to the starry California night sky and breathed in deeply.

Maybe he would watch *Enter the Dragon* tonight.

As he walked to his car he now remembered something else Bruce Lee said in that movie: *Don't think. FEEL. It is like a finger pointing a way to the moon. Do not concentrate on the finger or you will miss all that heavenly glory.*

 55

Chance and Madison sat in rocking chairs on her front porch in the leafy little neighborhood high up a hill at the edge of Santa Monica. It was late, and a full moon gave the trees on the street a mystical, deep green glow, like looking into a deep green forest path in England.

Madison had placed two hot cups of chamomile tea on the round white wicker table between their chairs. There was also a small plate of orange and almond oatmeal cookies. Would Chance have one? Was he a health fanatic? A sand-speckled cream and maroon candle burned brightly on the table causing shades of flickering light to play across Madison's sun-burned face. Chance could see the gold flecks in her blue eyes that only seemed to come out at night.

"So how do you know where to go?" said Madison. "If all we know is that he made a call from a pay phone outside the Coors ball park, how is that enough?"

Chance took a cookie from the plate. He ate half of one and looked at Madison.

"Wow. Did you make these?"

"Yes."

"What are they?"

"Orange and almond oatmeal."

Chance finished the second half of his cookie and took another.

"So you'll do a stake out?" said Madison.

"Modified, yes, maybe."

"What if he sees you first?"

"He won't. I have a sweat jacket with a hood. I have dark glasses. It worked for the Unabomber, and it will work for me."

"That's quite a role model."

"He escaped detection for years."

"And what happens when you do find him?"

"He and I talk."

"And if he doesn't want to talk?"

"He'll talk."

"How do you know?"

"It's what I do."

"How do you mean that?"

"*You* talked, didn't you?" said Chance.

Madison turned to him. She stopped rocking her chair.

"I don't know if I like that comparison."

"You talked about yourself and your fears and your bag-lady visions."

"But this is so different. He's probably killed somebody. And I'm not enjoying the comparison."

"Okay, sorry," said Chance. "Very inappropriate comparison. I just meant to say that I have some experience, inside and outside police work, and I will use it."

"And you're sure you'll find him?"

"No."

"Then why fly to Denver and waste a whole trip?"

"It won't be wasted."

"Not even if you don't find him?"

"Not even if I don't find him."

"Why not?" said Madison.

"Because nothing's ever wasted. Life's too good for that."

"I'll have to trust that."

56

Gibbon had been watching real crime cases on TV ever since the suicide of Tom Dumar. His favorites were *20/20*, *Dateline* and *48 Hours Mystery*. He learned from those shows how easy it was for law enforcement to track cell phone records, so he chose to use the pay phone outside the ballpark to try to communicate with Susan. He was happy that there were pay phones still left in the world, and he knew it wouldn't be long before they, too, were replaced by some technology that only young people knew how to use.

He hated how youth was worshipped these days. No wonder they're worshipped, he thought. They have all the money. Parents don't have time for parenting so they just give kids money. *I should talk.* Gibbon thought back on all the money he'd given his own son Gary.

Gibbon hated his own memories of childhood. He was teased in school. Kids called him "Glen Glutton" because he ate so much all day. Gibbon's thoughts turned to the buffalo meatloaf he'd had for lunch. Maybe he would have that for dinner, too. He got off the bare mattress on his bed and looked at his little black digital clock with red glowing numbers: 4:54. Time for dinner? Too early?

He wondered about how they got the meat of buffalo. He thought the Indians had killed them all. He put on his shoes and found his wallet on the dresser.

She said she would come for him.

When he called in his new name and address to her cell phone voice mail he knew that was the one and only call he was supposed to make. That was their agreement.

Gibbon walked into the hall to the elevator. Would it be days before she came or weeks? He asked her that more than once. She said probably days, maybe weeks, but probably days. He told her if it was months he wasn't going. She said certainly not months.

Down on the street Gibbon felt slightly out of breath. He remembered that they called Denver "the mile high city" so there wasn't as much air to breathe. He hated that. He walked the seven blocks to the little café that served his buffalo. Next to the café was a large newsstand. He felt his heart quicken. He might find the LA paper there. He wasn't supposed to communicate with anyone in LA but she couldn't stop him from reading the paper.

According to the paper, the two people still being held and now charged with arson for the fire that started in Laurel Canyon were Rico Hornsby and Garon Gibbon.

When God asked Abraham to sacrifice his son, Abraham obliged.

When Susan Dumar asked Gibbon to do the same, he was beyond caring. But some hope for humankind had been touched off in him by that woman. Something beyond heaven worth living for. All the hurts and pains made good. But could a magnetic woman of class really be that drawn to *him*?

He had bet his life on it.

And taking a seat in a booth in the Hungry Bronco Café, Gibbon felt like a gambler in the old west. Gambling his life away. He was like Doc Holliday! Maybe he would feel like a real man for the first time.

57

"Why, again, exactly are you going to Denver?" Madison asked, "Why not let Mossi's people do tracing and tracking and see if cell calls or even my internet probes turn something up?"

Chance reached for another orange and almond oatmeal cookie.

"I enjoy the hunt," he said "I enjoy being directly involved. Sometimes you can just set technology aside and go find someone. It's often simpler."

"Do you think he's just going to sit down and confess everything?"

"You never know."

"What will you ask him? What approach will you use?"

"I never know. When I know that, it limits things."

"How, then, can I learn from you? If you don't know what you're doing."

"You'll learn better from yourself. By what *you* try. You've already learned a lot."

Madison moved her chair back a little to get a better look at him.

"Are you afraid of death?" she said.

Chance laughed and put his hand up to contain the cookie fragment coming out of his mouth.

"No, are you?" he said.

"Of course I am. Tell me why you're not."

"I'm no more afraid of death than I am of the delta brain wave."

"Here we go again. As if I knew what that meant."

"It's easy. When you sleep and you descend to the deepest sleep level, the dreamless sleep, you are in delta. You don't know the world exists. You don't know *you* exist. You sleep like a newborn baby and you love it. How could death be any worse than that?"

"Well, all the same. I hope you don't find some kind of permanent newborn baby brain when you're in Denver."

"I doubt if our Mr. Gibbon is all that dangerous."

"It's not just him. There has to be something bigger than him running this... whatever this is. Someone much more evil and dangerous. You *know* that. Try to remember that there is already one dead person here so I'm not being unreasonable to worry about you. I think I would prefer that this investigation be accomplished electronically."

"There will be room for that too."

58

Chance contacted his coaching clients for the next ten days and moved their appointments into the future. He so rarely did anything like that, they were happy to accommodate him.

Would this mission take more than ten days? He didn't think so. It wasn't as if Glen Gibbon was a master spy with a new identity living in an obscure country. He had placed a call from outside Coors Field. He would be in that area. If Chance were Gibbon he'd wonder where the nearest pay phone was and then see one, perhaps, outside his window. Guessing again, but a good place to start.

Chance wouldn't mind being wrong about these guesses. He learned things when he was wrong. It allowed him to start over in newer, better directions.

On the plane ride in from LA to Denver, Chance read from his tattered copy of the essays of Ralph Waldo Emerson. Emerson was his favorite philosopher, having discovered his essays when he was a rookie cop. They gave him strength and philosophical stability. A solid place to come from.

Now on this flight he was enjoying seeing the parts he had highlighted when he was younger. In the essay called "Self-Reliance," he noticed he had underlined Emerson's words, "Society everywhere is a conspiracy against the manhood of every one of its members."

He remembered reading that essay when he was trying to understand the youth gangs in South LA. How easily gang members saw society, civilization and education as a conspiracy against their manhood. And how gang membership became a promise to give them their manhood back.

But how to understand Gibbon? Would Gibbon find his own manhood in his collection of telephoto shots of Susan Dumar sunning herself in the wooden deck of her Laurel Canyon cabin? A dark voyeuristic knight leering his way into the forest in search of Guinevere?

That might explain how vicious Gibbon had become in his negotiations with Tom Dumar. He never simply wanted a fair agreement. He always had to "win" and humiliate Tom. Chance had coached Tom to stand strong and disengage emotionally. Tom had done so well that Chance had marveled at how strong he was becoming. That's the primary reason why the suicide made no sense. He had worked his share of suicide scenes as a cop, and in even the most rudimentary investigations a rapid drop in self-esteem was always a factor.

Tom's self-esteem has been rising, his inner strength growing more solid with each bold action he took. Tom was almost becoming reckless at times in what he was attempting, but Chance enjoyed seeing it.

As the plane landed Chance put his book of essays into his leather carrying case and pulled his hotel information out of his folder. He had booked a room for a week at the Oxford Hotel, less than half a mile away from the ballpark. He looked forward to his time in Denver. Surveillances were always profound times for him. While his buddies on the force found them to be boring, he had great experiences. Watching a home or building throughout the night had given him a strange, exalted form of consciousness.

Like a cat sitting in front of a mouse hole.

That kind of attentiveness always lifted Chance. He liked hanging out in the space between thoughts. Prior to his stakeout experiences he had been a young man practically eaten alive by his own thoughts. Thought clusters flew into his mind like geese flying into an airplane's jet engine. Flocks of negative thoughts about why society produced criminals and why the courts and media favored the outlaws and dismissed the victims.

His stakeout experiences ended all that.

Now he was able to relax and focus and see a force of good running the universe. He would be a part of that force, a knight, almost. A blue knight with a badge advancing against… against what? Emerson's words said it best, "Let us advance on chaos and the dark."

Chance was glad to be in the Denver airport again. He'd had a case once that took him to Denver once a month for almost a year. He admired the foresight of the city planners who put the airport at a good distance from the urban center of Denver. The previous airport's location had become dangerous to Denver's residents and businesses. Chance's whole professional life had been about reducing danger to citizens, and he appreciated it when others took up the same cause. He liked it that this location would allow for growth in the Denver area, and that future generations would be better served.

The trains to the baggage area were clean, swift and efficient. And Denver's airport was downright luxuriant, with shops, restaurants, and all the conveniences of an upscale mall. Just being in this airport gave Chance a good feeling. No other airport he knew of had so much interesting internal architecture and art exhibits.

To Chance it was like landing inside an affirmation of the best that civilization had to offer.

His cab ride to the Oxford Hotel gave him a chance to go through his phone messages. There was a text from his sister Nikki thanking him for going to the reading. It ended with "thumbs up on your new friend."

He felt a slight butterfly in his stomach when he saw that, having been very happy with his ability to keep his relationship with Madison on a friendly, professional level so far. It made him nervous that his sister could see more to the relationship than he was willing to admit was there. His sister was like those "precogs" in that bad Tom Cruise science fiction movie that he could never remember the name of. The precogs were cute young women with short-cropped Peter Pan hair and they could see the future. That was Nikki.

Chance saw that the cab was turning onto 17th Street, where the Oxford was, just five blocks from the ballpark. He looked out the window and once again admired Denver's renovated lower downtown neighborhood with charming old world restaurants, galleries, bookstores and those old brick buildings that took the mind back into the late 1800s during the height of Denver's silver rush. This was Denver as he remembered it.

What he didn't expect to see was Glen Gibbon. Not now, not this soon. But it was surely Gibbon himself outside a café whose window featured "Buffalo Meatloaf: Denver's Best!"

Gibbon had his back turned now, with short grey and brown hair coming out from under a green floppy hat, purchasing a newspaper from an old black man at a sidewalk stand. At least it looked like Gibbon. And it looked like he was arguing over the change he was given and the whole involved scene gave Chance time to put his sunglasses on inside the cab and raise his hood.

Never let your guard down. Like a cat in front of a mouse hole.

The cab rolled down the street to the hotel and Gibbon was soon out of sight. Chance felt no anxiety. He now knew Gibbon was in this neighborhood and that he would find him.

He walked into the Oxford's hotel lobby feeling upbeat. His guesses were correct. Gibbon was living nearby. Was it a huge coincidence that he already saw him? No, given his prediction that he'd be living near the pay phone he called Susan from. And so now it would just be a matter of time. Chance admired the European antiques that decorated the old world lobby of the Oxford and rode the elevator up to his room. Inserting his plastic card in the slot, he opened the door and took in the elegant room. The bed was king sized and the view of downtown was perfect.

This is where the cat would sleep.

59

Madison's morning walk through her leafy Santa Monica neighborhood took her down to Arizona Street where her favorite farmer's market was opening for business. She had brought an empty canvas bag and began to look for her usual selection of carrots, potatoes, and onions.

Right now suicide was the furthest thing from her mind.

"These are all picked fully ripe," said a smiling old woman who looked like she was straight from the British countryside, grey bun-wrapped hair and flush cheeks with dancing eyes. She must have been in her eighties, but who could tell anymore? Madison was in a cheerful but inquisitive mood.

"Why does *that* matter so much?" she asked the woman as she searched for her wallet to find money to pay. "That they are picked fully ripe?"

The old woman was happy to talk.

"Oh, deary," she said, and was the accent Irish? It seemed like no one in Santa Monica actually grew up here like Madison. "Aren't you a pretty one. Are you in the movies?"

"No, no."

"Pickin' fully ripe is *most* important. All my produce is brought here within twenty-four hours of the pickin'! That lets the flavor develop."

"How's that different from the produce in other stores?"

"Those items? They are grown for toughness. Duration. Not flavor. It's a mass market for them. But the good life is about being selective, isn't it? Patient. We plant small quantities, so we can experiment."

Madison smiled and nodded. Life lessons were showing up everywhere, it seemed. This woman had a good formula: Be simple. Be patient. Be selective.

What if she let her life be like this lady's philosophy? Full of flavor and experiment? No more rushing around. Be selective! No more scooting here and there chasing... chasing what? Love. Love and money. Both.

In her chasing days she would have settled for either love *or* money. She knew they weren't the same thing, but each one represented security. Or so she thought back then.

She gathered her bulging bag up and began her walk back up the hill to her neighborhood. She thought back again on her previous life of chasing. It reminded her of Steve Martin's movie about LA—especially the scene in which Steve Martin roller skates through the art gallery, sailing past the paintings of the masters. That was her past life. If you move fast enough from job to job, from person to person, you don't have to sit with your own mind and realize how unhappy you are.

Meeting and working with Robert Chance had stopped all that racing around. It was a lifelong habit that she thought was a permanent part of her personality. Her parents had even called her "Scooter" when she was little. Chance slowed her down so that she could be introduced to something still and peaceful inside her.

What was it, exactly?

Her soul?

She gave up trying to think and slowed her walk down a bit as she approached her block because it looked like her car's windshield was shattered. It must be an optical illusion. The sycamores and the sun shafts were always playing visual tricks.

As she got closer she saw it was really shattered, and it looked like a corner of the driver's seat was torn away. A gun shot? In broad daylight? With no one in the car?

She stopped a hundred feet away and looked around. No one. Birds were singing. Everything seemed peaceful. She walked slowly toward the car. It looked very much like a gunshot had done this. But why? Random kids during a drive by? That didn't seem likely. Not this neighborhood and not in the morning. That would be more likely at night, under the cover of darkness, during surges of alcohol or whatever else.

Madison gingerly pushed some of the glass crystals loose. She picked one up. She held the jagged, translucent nugget of glass up to the sun and let a rainbow prism form on her tanned forearm.

Chance would think this was beautiful.

She shooed a scrub jay off the hood of her car.

She wondered what to do next.

911?

Was this an emergency?

She heard a buzzing sound from her purse and decided she'd answer her phone first, then choose her next move. It was from a number she didn't recognize so she let it go to voice mail and looked around her neighborhood again.

Silence.

Solitude.

Did this really happen?

She went inside her house. She went to the phone on the wall. Call 911? No. She pulled out her cell. She would call Chance. He'd know what to do. And he might also have an opinion about whether this was random.

Chance didn't answer the call, but as she was putting her phone away she saw that he was calling her right back.

Madison said, "Hi. Thanks. You're there in Denver okay?"

"Yes. I'm at the Oxford and I've already had a sighting of our target, if you can believe that."

"Gibbon already? You *are* good."

"Just lucky. What's going on there?"

"My windshield was shot at, shattered. It happened this morning. I was on my walk."

"*Shot* at? Are you sure?"

"Yes, it tore through the top of my front seat."

"Any note or message or anything? Anyone see it?"

"I don't know of anything. You know my neighborhood. It's strange. Just silent."

"If it was a message, there will *be* a message. If it was random… well, I don't know… did you check your home phone for message?"

"Not yet. I'll do that. Then call who? 911? Mossi?"

"Call Mossi. Tell him you're working with me and that I'm out of town."

"You really want him that involved right now?"

"I think so. He's got this whole thing as an arson deal anyway. Stay with that when you talk to him. He doesn't need to know why I'm in Denver or even that I'm here. He'll call me if he wants and I'll deal with it."

"Let me check my phone and my email and I'll call you right back."

Madison walked through her house. She looked around for signs of entry or disturbance. There were none. She put her cell down on the kitchen counter and took the phone off the wall. There was a beeping sound on the line signifying a message waiting. She punched in some numbers and waited. She heard a muted odd voice, as if someone were speaking through tinfoil. Was it a Boston accent?

"This is a message for Little Miss Snoopy. We are sorry you weren't in your car this morning when we came to see you. Time for you and your cop boyfriend to back off and shut down. Repeat: Back off and shut down."

Madison punched the 9 key to save the message and called Chance back. She repeated the message for Chance and gave him her number and code so he could call and listen to it himself.

Chance said, "Okay, let's do it this way. Call 911 and have a patrol officer come take your statement and write up a report. I'll call Mossi myself right now so he can give his patrol a heads-up on finding the bullet and talking to your neighbors. Do you have anywhere you can go stay?"

"I'm not going anywhere," said Madison. "How can I do this work if on my first case I run and hide?"

"Well, I'm not sure I like you staying there."

"You don't have to like it. Besides it was your decision to fly off to Denver and chase down some loser while the real dangerous people are here shooting at *me*."

"You're making me feel cowardly."

"Good! Stay in touch."

"Don't worry."

60

Chance put his sunglasses on as he stepped into the elevator on the fifth floor of the Oxford Hotel. As he reached the first floor lobby he also pulled his sweatshirt hood over his head. Not even his sister would recognize him now as he walked into the cool, fresh, thin air of Denver's lower downtown.

He couldn't get Madison's shattered windshield out of his mind. What was she onto that they knew she was onto that made them do that? And who were *they* if Gibbon is here?

He would take a slow walk around the ballpark and make sure he circled back to visit the newsstand where he saw Gibbon. Or should he be calling him Brock Young? Right before he left his hotel room, he'd called the front desk on a whim, asking if he could speak to another hotel guest named Brock Young. The operator said there was no such guest. Never hurts to try everything.

But he thought an apartment or loft rental would be more likely. Change of identity usually meant more permanent re-location.

The long slow walk gave Chance time to think about one gunshot and Madison's green Volvo. Who could that be if Gibbon was in Denver and his son was in custody? What other players were there? What had Mossi said about seeing Susan talking to a man in a car after the funeral?

His head was wrapped in bandages. He was on foot. I sent my partner after him while I tailed Mrs. Dumar. The phantom of the opera walked into Wal-Mart and we never saw him again.

Chance found the newsstand and talked to the old African American man he saw arguing with Gibbon. He grabbed a Denver newspaper and reached in his pocket for money. "How are the Rockies doing?" he said.

"Not good," said the old man.

"What's their problem?"

"Pitchers. They can't get good pitchers here. They hate it."

"Why is that?"

"It's the thin air at this altitude. You hit a ball and it just flies. There is no air to stop it. It's like hitting a ball on the moon. No pitcher likes that."

Chance nodded. He'd known about the high scores at Coors Field. Get behind by six runs and you're still in the game. Chance thought it sounded like fun.

"I saw a redheaded guy…" said Chance, "fairly heavy guy, in a green floppy hat arguing with you yesterday."

"Oh yes indeed, the jerk. He didn't want to pay! He said he shouldn't pay full price for the paper he was buying because it was late in the day and he said it was an old paper. I couldn't believe the fool. Never had that happen before. He says I'm not paying full price for old news!"

"Have you seen him around here?"

"Eats over there. That café." The news vendor pointed to the café that advertised buffalo meat. "Every day I see him. I think every day. Almost every day."

"Thank you," said Chance. He handed the man a twenty-dollar bill. "Can you keep our talk confidential? Just between you and me?"

"Well yes sir, yes. Are you police?"

"Just a concerned citizen."

"I got your back."

"Thanks."

Chance looked across the street from the Gibbon café and saw a coffee shop there. He walked down to the traffic light, crossed the street and went in, and took a seat by the window.

He was on his third cup of coffee and second blueberry muffin and still there was no sign of Gibbon entering the café across the street that served buffalo meatloaf. This could take awhile, he thought, as his phone vibrated in his pocket. He answered while leaving a clump of dollars on the table and walked outside. He headed north on Wynkoop Street.

"This is Chance."

"Sergeant Mossi here. I'm in a meeting so I don't have much time."

"Talk anyway."

"I met your friend or assistant... whatever... Miss Kerr, Madison, the one with the blue eyes, the beautiful..."

"I know who you mean, yes."

"My God, Chance. How many auditions did you do till you found *her*?"

"She was a friend. Please continue."

"We talked to her neighbors about the gunshot, and they saw an orange van drive by after hearing the shots."

"An orange van. Driven by whom?"

"They couldn't tell. The witnesses were a husband and wife walking a dog. The husband said the driver had a bandage on his forehead. The wife disagreed."

"Okay," said Chance. "Any bullets found?"

"We've got the one and I'll have more for you on that later. Where are you, Chance?"

"Vacationing."

"I'll bet."

"I'll be back soon enough. Any idea who this orange van could belong to?"

"You tell *me*. I liked Susan Dumar for the arson, and it looks like she met a new friend after the funeral. The bandage matches. You tell me."

"I'll tell you when I get back. I'll give you some guesses but that's all I've got."

"Your friend gets shot at and you're on vacation? This doesn't work for me."

"That's why you're detective, and obviously a good one. And, please, she herself wasn't shot at."

"Warned off, then. I heard the voice message on her phone. She played it for me"

"Do you have anything else?"

"Not yet. Call me when you're back."

"That I'll do."

Chance hung up and kept walking north on Wynkoop. He decided to walk in widening circles around the meatloaf café and the ballpark. He'd keep his eyes open for Gibbon and do some thinking as well.

61

Gibbon had set his pill bottles in a neat row on the shelf below the mirror in the bathroom. He loved looking at them. Pretty maids, all in a row, ready to serve him. He then thought of a song he sang as a little boy. *Down by the station, early in the morning. See the little pufferbellies all in a row.*

He made a mental note to put the little pufferbellies away when Susan came. She might not want to know that he was taking medication for anxiety.

He lit the scented candle in the glass jar on his toilet. Evergreen. Smells of our most joyous season.

In a perfect world Brock Young would not be an anxious man.

Gibbon's doctor had asked him whether his anxiety was social. Gibbon said he didn't know what that meant, and his doctor patiently explained that some people became anxious in social gatherings, at parties, or in meetings of any kind. Gibbon had said yes. That was definitely happening. There was tightness in his chest and a knot in his stomach in those situations. Breathing had become difficult.

As Gibbon described those experiences to his doctor, he noticed that a silver fountain pen was already scratching out a prescription for social anxiety medication.

The doctor then asked when else Gibbon felt his symptoms.

"When I'm alone," he said. "When I'm by myself at night or even alone in my office. I start to sweat. I feel so isolated. I feel a kind of ominous feeling. You know the feeling?"

The doctor shook his head no and asked if what he felt was impending doom. He explained to Gibbon that a sense of impending doom was a specific indicative psycho-pharmaceutical symptom. Gibbon said that yes, that was it exactly. He was glad to have a name for it.

"Does the medication remove the *sense* of it," said Gibbon, "Or does it remove the doom itself?"

The doctor stared at Gibbon, not knowing if he was serious.

"The whole point here Mr. Gibbon is biochemical. We deal with everything on that level. Any external doom, real or not, would not itself be treated by the medication."

There was more scratching from the silver fountain pen, and Gibbon got his second prescription.

He stared at the bottles now as he was remembering that doctor's visit. He went back to his bedroom to get his small bottle of chocolate milk that had grown warm. He returned to the bathroom and took a pill from each container.

He felt a wave of disgust.

He realized his anxiety symptoms only occurred when he was alone or with somebody.

He laughed bitterly after he swallowed both pills down and went back into his bedroom to watch TV. TV was a good friend now. TV was his way of not being alone while being alone.

There was a special true crime show on about a man who had disappeared for ten years before his daughter decided to search for him. In the past, Gibbon used to mock his wife for watching these shows, but these days he couldn't get enough of them.

He grabbed his notebook from his bedside table and clicked his mechanical pencil into ready mode.

You never know what you might learn.

 **62**

Chance woke up the next morning when the streaks of sun came through the gauze curtains in his hotel room. He went to the bathroom and splashed cold water on his face. He resisted the temptation to fire up his little coffee machine and went right to the carpet for his morning ritual of thirty pushups and fifty sit-ups. He hated doing it but loved how he felt when it was over.

And it felt so good to do them without Wu Li pressing on his back.

He rolled over on the floor and stared at the ceiling. There was something he couldn't get out of his mind that Madison had said. Now he didn't know for sure whether he might have dreamed it. She had been saying something about the calamondin orange tree she owned.

So what? They were just talking about orange trees and lemon trees in Chance's yard.

He took the elevator down to the Oxford Hotel lobby and stepped into the streets of Denver. He put his sunglasses on, put his hood up and walked. Why didn't he just stop the cab and follow Gibbon the first time he saw him? Chance didn't work that way. Chance worked in circles. Wu Li had taught him that. Never push the river. Just go with the river.

He circled the entire structure of Coors Field passing the same pay phones Gibbon must have used. At one pay phone he stopped and looked up and around. High on a building down Blake Street near Broadway and 24th he saw the sign "Ballpark Lofts." That was a true possibility.

He walked a number of blocks down Blake to the newsstand and saw the old man he'd given the twenty-dollar bill to. The man saw him coming and began nodding his head. Chance looked around and then walked up to him.

"He's in there now," said the man. "I was hoping you'd come by. He has been in there for an hour. They open at six for breakfast."

Chance looked the other way and then bought a Denver newspaper. When he paid the man, there was an extra twenty in his hand. Without saying anything he crossed the street to an RTD bus bench two blocks away. He sat on the bench and pulled his hood around his ears. His eyes remained fixed on the café door.

Now we were getting somewhere.

 63

Madison met Sandy Redfield, the surfer dude private eye, at a Bubba Gump shrimp stand near the end of the Santa Monica pier. He had called her twice with "an idea" about the Laurel Canyon fire and wanted to talk.

Madison had been to a client meeting that morning and was in her business skirt and blouse but had changed her shoes from flat heels to white tennis shoes. She didn't care how it looked, or that the trend—wearing your running shoes with your business clothes—had gone out with the eighties.

In her previous life she would have been very intrigued with Sandy Redfield and cared a lot about how she looked. He was cute and seemed like a great dad to his kid. She also liked his wild and free life and how he didn't give up his surfing to do business in investigations.

"I told you I had my sources," Sandy said after they both were served their orders of golden fried shrimp in red plastic baskets with butcher paper taking in the tasty greases. He noticed Madison staring at her basket and tentatively removing a shrimp and looking at it. He said, "This shrimp is steamed in beer. Isn't it great?"

"It looks great. But what about your sources."

"My sources say that the woman is behind everything. The poor widow has been observed conducting herself in suspicious ways. Not consistent with sadness."

"Okay, we've kind of passed that marker ourselves, so that's not new information right now," said Madison. "Although I'm really glad you contacted me. Do you know any more than that?"

"She bought a used orange van three days ago at a buy-here/pay-here lot. She paid cash and used her own name, like she didn't care much about hiding her actions."

"Like she might be going away soon anyway."

"Exactly."

"Remind me of why you care so much about this arson case."

"I told you already. Laurel Canyon. It's where the music died. The Byrds. Mama Cass."

"Right, right."

"And then there's you," Sandy said.

"Me?"

"I care about the music, but I care about you, too. How you were coming to my place, going in to see my boss, how brave you are to want to do this work. I just wanted something good to happen for you."

"I'm very grateful for that."

"It's like teaching someone to surf. You want them to get up on the board so badly and you know how hard it is at the start. You want to take that learning part away but you can't."

"They have to fall."

"They have to wipe out, again and again."

"That's comforting."

"But, no, not always, though! Sometimes some young dude just gets up and rides along the water like he was in slow motion, born to ride."

"I like that better."

"That's what it felt like with you."

"Did you teach Ben to surf?"

"When he was three."

"Really?"

"You start on the sand. Teach them to do their pop-ups on the sand. Then gently into the whitewash. No real waves at the beginning. And you're always there encouraging once you're in the water, body surfing next to him. Having him choose it and seeing that he loves it."

"You sound like an amazing father. Ben is lucky to have you."

"It's more like the other way around."

After a long time of eating in silence passed, Madison looked for a trash can to put her basket, paper, and shrimp tails in.

"Does this work ever get really dangerous?" she said. "For the investigator?"

"Almost never," he said. "You are the last person bad characters want to bring harm to. In a way, law enforcement considers you to be on their team. Doing something to a cop or an investigator would bring the wrath of God down on these creepy people and they know that. They don't want that."

"I'm glad."

"I'm sensing there's a point to your question."

"My car was shot at. The windshield was blown out, and there was a bullet in the driver's seat."

Sandy sat back and brushed a lot of blonde hair back up off his forehead.

"Whoa," he said.

Madison searched his sunburned face for a further reaction.

"Whoa?"she said. "That's quite a response. Do you mean like, 'Whoa,' stop investigating' or 'Whoa, that's cool'?"

Sandy said, "Well, whoa, that's pretty cool. I mean it must be scary, too. But notice that you weren't in the car. So it's pretty cool."

"Cool, okay, in what way?"

"It means no matter what marker you think you're on in this game, you are probably getting close to something even you don't know about."

"I'm thinking that, too."

"So do you feel safe? Did it happen at your home?"

"Yes. And no. Or rather, no and yes. I don't feel totally safe, and I'm angry. They think they can scare me because I'm a girl."

"You want to stay with Ben and me?"

Madison looked at Sandy for a moment too long. She shook her head, no. But the idea was more interesting than she wanted it to be.

"You can change your mind any time," said Sandy.

"I'm going to hold my ground for now and thank you."

They got up to walk back down the pier to the highway. Their small talk went from raising children to keeping investigation time journals, and neither one of them seemed to want the meeting to end. Finally they reached the walking park that runs along Ocean Avenue. Madison reached out to shake his hand.

"Any last words of advice?" she said.

"Okay. Yes." Sandy Redfield looked like he didn't know whether to say this or not. He decided to say it.

"When you look for motives, keep these two rules of thumb in mind. These were taught to me early by my boss and mentor Marquis Boston."

"And these rules are?"

"Men want love and women want money."

Madison stopped walking. "Oh, that's flattering."

"It's not supposed to be; it's just a guide to criminal motivation. Notice how men freak out when they get dumped or rejected. Notice what women will do for money."

Madison blushed a little and said, "That's such a gross generalization and such stereotyping that I can't possibly take it seriously."

"I knew I liked you," said Sandy and they waved to each other as they took their separate ways.

 64

Gibbon had a funny feeling that he was being watched as he emerged from his café and turned to walk back to his loft. He even stopped to look around a little bit to see if he could spot the source of his strange feeling.

He could.

It was that old black man at the newsstand staring at him like he was some kind of criminal.

Give it up, old man. I just argued with you about paying full price for yesterday's news. They mark bread down when it goes stale, why not news?

Satisfied that he'd found the source of his creepy feeling, Gibbon kept walking toward his ballpark loft. Later today he would be buying some sheets and blankets and other furnishings, but for now he just wanted to get back to his pills. Most of his life he had bragged about never taking alcohol or drugs into his system. His church had also disallowed it, but these drugs were different. They kept him from going crazy. They gave him the patience he needed to have the rest of his story get played out. They kept him from doubting everything.

He passed through the lobby of his building still feeling a little strange. Could the newspaper vendor be following him? That didn't make sense. He was starting to get really anxious now and felt like he couldn't get a full breath.

A security guard came around the corner in the lobby, and Gibbon's heart started pounding like a hammer.

"Having a nice day?" the guard smiled as he got on the elevator with Gibbon. Gibbon considered stepping off and letting the guard ride alone, but that would look too weird. The whole point of being Brock Young in Denver was to *not* be weird anymore.

"It's a *great* day," said Gibbon in a voice he didn't recognize. It was high-pitched, almost like he had taken in helium. Why hadn't he taken his social anxiety medicine to breakfast with him? It had even said on the bottle to take it with food. He couldn't stop talking.

"You know what?" said Gibbon to the guard, "If I was any happier I'd have to be twins!"

Was he yelling? Should he have said that? He'd have to be twins?

The guard smiled a little but slowly stepped back into the corner of the elevator.

Gibbon still couldn't stop talking.

"Are you armed?" he said to the guard in as friendly a voice as he could find.

The guard instinctively reached to his belt where a black leather cylinder of something was.

Gibbon looked at it. "What is that? Mace?"

The guard said, "We're not supposed to talk about that. These are just lofts and condos here. It's not a prison. We aren't really even needed. It's just that the residents appreciate us."

"I admire law enforcement," said Gibbon. "Of any kind I mean, I know you're not law enforcement. But still, any authority I admire. Rule of law, and all of that."

The guard's floor arrived and he stepped out the elevator door quickly saying to Gibbon, "I hope you enjoy the place you have here, sir."

"You, too!" said Gibbon as the door started to close.

Gibbon put his hand out to open the doors again.

He couldn't believe he had said that. He called out to the guard, "I mean I know you probably don't have a place here, but I meant for you to enjoy your time on patrol or guarding, and all your work here. Enjoy *that*."

The door slammed and the elevator started to rise again toward Gibbon's floor.

Never again, he vowed to himself. Never again do you leave your loft without medication. It would not be a great thing for Susan to ask for Brock Young and have everyone's facial expression say, *You mean the weirdo?*

65

Gibbon's refrigerator had enough chocolate milk left to take his pills with, but he'd have to make another grocery run soon. He'd considered going on a *chocolate-milk-only* diet until Susan arrived so that Brock Young would be trim for her, but there must have been something in the medication that made him unbelievably hungry at all times.

He washed down his pills and put some extras in his pocket for good measure for when he went out.

He turned on his TV and decided to kick back a bit and let the pills take over. Then he'd go out and shop some more for his loft.

What kind of prints could he put up on the walls that would impress her the most? He had seen a discount art store on one of his walks around the ballpark. He was certain that if they were already calling themselves a discount store he could work his bartering skills on them to reduce the prices even more.

Not that he needed to do that.

He'd pulled all his money out of his LA banks when he left and put most of it in a Brock Young account at the Bank of the West on 17th Street.

Gibbon woke from his drug-induced nap with a start at the gunfire sounds on his TV. They were doing a simulation of a shooting on a true-crime show and somehow the gunshots had entered Gibbon's dream, and as he sat up on his bed he clutched his chest to feel for wounds or blood. He shook his head and went to the bathroom to wash up.

Time to buy some real nice art.

Maybe Glen Gibbon didn't have much class but Brock Young would. She would be pleasantly surprised on her first visit to his loft. Was that days away? Weeks? She told him to be patient, and that it would be sooner than he realized.

His mother used to tell him things like that.

Be patient, Glen. Maybe someday, Glen. We'll see!

As his elevator ride reached the lobby floor he was glad that the medication was in him and giving him that expanded, slow-motion feeling, like walking through clear gelatin. The whole world was moving more slowly.

As he stepped into the lobby he noticed a man in a far corner lounge chair looking directly at him.

Or *was* he looking at him?

It was hard to tell because the man had a hooded sweatshirt on that partially obscured his face. He was also wearing sunglasses.

Gibbon decided to pay him no mind but stopped short as he was about to enter the revolving doors when the man said, "Glen Gibbon, I can't believe it's you."

Gibbon stepped back, looked around the lobby and noticed that the lady at the main desk had looked up and raised her eyebrows. He also noticed a feeling of extreme pressure on his chest, like a giant paw was pressing on it. What kind of paw? The paw of a polar bear? It was pressing his chest in as he tried to answer.

"You must be mistaken," he said as he tried to smile but the muscles in his face weren't working. Damn these pills, he thought; I am out of control at a time when I need control.

The hooded man stood up and extended his hand to Gibbon.

"Brock Young, then. Sorry, Brock, I had you mixed up with a guy I know named Gibbon."

Gibbon then saw who it was.

It was Chance, Tom Dumar's nosy coach. How could this be happening? Gibbon suddenly wished his TV dream had been real and he'd been mercifully shot in the chest and left to die peacefully on his bed upstairs.

"We've got to talk, Brock," said Chance. "Catch up. How about your place? Anywhere else wouldn't be private enough, don't you agree?"

Gibbon stood motionless and looked over again at the woman behind the desk who was staring at the whole encounter. He broke into a big grin and called out to her, "Old friend!"

He turned to Chance and motioned toward the elevator and both men nodded to the woman and smiled at her as they walked past her desk.

Just two old friends running into each other in Denver.

 **66**

Chance took a chair at the table in Gibbon's kitchen and asked if there was any coffee or water.

"Don't drink coffee," said Gibbon. "There's a little chocolate milk left and water from the tap."

Chance stood up and took a plastic amber colored glass from a cabinet. It was the only one there. He looked at Gibbon and Gibbon nodded. Chance filled the glass with water and sat back down.

"Sit down, Glen," he said.

Gibbon did not sit down. He tried to find his focus inside a sense of fear and confusion. Might this be the end of the whole thing?

"Your son is in jail, Glen. But you knew that. In fact I'm willing to bet that you even knew that would happen before it happened."

Gibbon said nothing.

"Your son won't talk yet, but that was before this. That was before I found you. This changes everything, can you see that, Glen?"

Gibbon remained standing in the opening between the kitchen and the living room.

"You might as well sit down, Glen, because I'm not going away."

Gibbon stared at Chance for a long time and then cautiously sat down.

"I'm not the police, Glen. I'm someone who's here to talk to you. You don't have a lot of people like that in your life right now, so I wouldn't waste this opportunity if I were you."

Gibbon felt like he was losing consciousness.

He pulled a handkerchief out of his back pocket and dabbed the sweat on the back of his neck. How much did Chance know? If he was here and calling me Brock Young, it must be a lot.

Gibbon said, "I know your type, Chance. You have no morals, you have no God, you have no church, and yet you're better than everyone and you've got everything figured out."

Chance smiled and took a drink of water. Pretty good for tap water. He always liked being in Denver.

"You are wrong about every one of those things," said Chance. "So therefore you obviously don't know my type."

Gibbon nodded sarcastically.

Chance continued, "My big question here is whether you know Susan Dumar's type. Do you have that all wrong, too? Because I say you do. If you are here in Denver under the name Brock Young like some new life is going to happen for you, you probably guessed wrong about her, too."

"I don't even know her."

"Agreed!"

"I mean, literally."

"Oh, now, don't do that, Glen. Like my father used to tell me, you can't kid an old kidder. And I'm an old kidder from way back, so I can see right away that you are kidding me."

Gibbon said nothing.

"We have your computer, Glen. Or at least all the most interesting contents."

Gibbon felt his chest tighten again. He pulled the handkerchief back out and noticed that it was now cold and wet.

He took a deep breath, remembering that he'd deleted everything.

Chance said, "And I know what you're thinking. You're thinking you deleted everything. But that doesn't always work, Glen. You've heard about information being retrieved after deleting? Right? How else would I be here, knowing your fantasy name?"

"Get to the point and then I'll be asking you to get out. This building has security.

"Security, yes, I've seen him. Very scary. Is that mace he carries or just a real big container of ChapStick?"

"What do you want from me?"

"I want a few answers, Glen, that's all, and then I'll leave and you can move out and change your name again and choose some new nightmare for yourself."

"What kind of answers?"

"What happened to my friend?"

"What friend? Oh. Your coaching client? Tom Dumar? You know what happened. It's a matter of record."

"Did you type the suicide email from his computer?"

"I don't know what you're talking about."

"Do you have problems with grammar, Glen? Did no one teach you the English language? Or maybe English is your second language."

Gibbon's left arm started to feel tingly. He tried to breathe deeply, but couldn't find the bottom of his lungs. He couldn't get his father's face out of his eyes. He had to look through him now to see Robert Chance sitting there.

"What was Susan going to do for you, Glen? Was she going to meet you here? Were you going to go somewhere together? Canada? Bermuda? Can you see how you've been played here, Glen? I'm the only one you can talk to right now in the whole world."

"My son is in jail. If he committed a crime so be it. What does this have to do with the woman or me? I read the LA paper. The arson case is closed. End of story. You can't accept that your friend, your client, committed suicide. I know your kind. Your kind hates to lose."

"She's got another man, Glen."

Gibbon felt a ringing in his ears. Then he felt a rush like the ocean. Like someone had taken two enormous sea shells and slammed them against his ears. Love conquers all, she once told him. Love conquers all. He felt like putting his hands to his ears and yelling that love conquers all. Damn this medication.

"It's true, Glen. She's been followed by the police. They're on to her. They caught her after the funeral with another man. Right there in her car, too, right outside of Wal-Mart. Sergeant Mossi himself saw it. He's a criminal investigator with LAPD. It's over for you, Glen. It was never even there for you. You have been used, my friend. And I say my friend because I'm the only friend you've got now."

Gibbon stood up and pulled his chair to a corner in the kitchen. He sat back down.

Gibbon said, "If you were right about any of this, you wouldn't be up here in Denver freelancing. You used to be a cop. You know the law. Things happen because of rules and law. People don't just travel around trying to solve things on their own, especially with no financial interest in it. You have no financial stake in any of this so I think you are suspect."

"You think I'd need to be making money to come up here? I think you're projecting, Glen. I think you are projecting you onto me. I don't care about money the same way you do. I care about finding the truth, and that's all."

"You want some kind of revenge for Susan killing your client."

"It's not revenge."

"What is it?"

"It's a reckoning."

Chance then decided to take a risk. He got up from the table, walked over to Gibbon, and put his arm around his shoulders. Gibbon stiffened, resisted, and then gave in. He allowed himself to be hugged. Chance said softly, "She saw you were lonely. She saw you were attracted to her. She decided to use you. Don't let it go any further. Stop covering for her. Start standing up for yourself. No one else ever has, but you can."

"What do you want me to do?" Gibbon wished right away he hadn't said that. He sounded like a little boy. He would *never* sound like that negotiating for a lower price on something.

Chance stepped back. "I want you to tell me the whole story."

"Then what?"

"Then I go away."

"You got police waiting outside."

"I do not."

"Your detective Mossi friend."

"Doesn't even know where I am."

"Why should I believe you?

"Think it through. Do you think if they were outside here to arrest you that they would let me, a civilian, come in here and do all this talking? They don't even have the same questions for you I have."

"How do you mean?"

"Mossi is looking at Susan Dumar for connection to the arson. Period. He's the one who *closed* the case on Tom's so-called suicide."

Gibbon thought it through, or tried to.

Was thinking even possible right now?

His mind was roaring like an ocean out of control. But what Chance was saying made sense. The police closed the case. He knew that. Everything had gone as planned.

"How do I know you'll go away?"

"Because I keep my word."

"How do I know you aren't wearing what is it… a wire?"

Chance held his hands out. He stood up slowly. He pulled his sweatshirt off. He then slowly pulled his black T-shirt up over his head and laid it on the kitchen table. Gibbon stared at Chance's bare arms and chest. Probably works out twice a day at one of those ego-flattering LA bodybuilding clubs. Chance pulled his sweat pants off and stood in his boxers.

He extended his arms out and turned around.

"I'm for total disclosure, Glen. I have nothing hidden at all. I'm in favor of both of us baring everything till we get to the truth."

Gibbon got up from his chair and picked up Chance's clothes and felt through them.

"Okay," he said. "She had me go into his office and send the email."

"So you killed him in his office that night."

"No, no, no. Tom was dead when I got there. Face down. Pool of blood. Weapon on the floor. I just did the final emailing. You can't get me for murder. You can't murder a man who's already dead."

"So she just wanted your prints all over there?"

"Whatever! She said she forgot to send the email. Originally, I was just to do the fire later. She panicked that night. She wanted to be away from the scene, I guess, so she couldn't go back in herself. I had to go in."

"Why would you want to run away with a woman who killed her husband and made it look like a suicide?"

"You'd never understand."

Chance slowly put his pants back on. He said, "Who's the man Susan met with after the funeral?"

"How would I know *that*? She was going to come here and be with me. I was a moron to trust her."

"And your son, and the arson?"

"I'm not going to give you any more of that. You've already got that."

"But that was her request?"

"Leave it at that."

Chance put his shirt back on.

"How are you feeling right now, Glen?"

"As if you cared."

"How about pretending I cared."

"I'm feeling the usual."

"Meaning?"

"This always happens to me. Some way or another. I trust someone, and this happens."

Chance set his plastic drinking glass on the counter by the sink. He put his sunglasses in his pocket. He wouldn't need those anymore. And the hooded sweatshirt he folded up to carry under his arm now. He wouldn't need that, either.

Gibbon felt strange watching him getting ready to go. Somehow, after having hated and feared this individual… he didn't want him to leave.

"What would *you* do?" he said to Chance. Chance turned back to look at him and held the door.

"Stop trusting people," he said.

"Oh, that's helpful. I thought you were one of these positive thinking coaches."

"I am. And I'm coaching you right now, Glen. Stop trusting people. Just trust yourself."

Gibbon hated the tears that came into his eyes and waved Chance out the door hoping his breakdown wouldn't be noticed.

He knew his life was over.

67

Chance realized on the flight in from Denver that he couldn't wait to see her.

Angie always waited for him.

He got her as a puppy when he left police work to set up his practice coaching people. Chance had always enjoyed helping people solve their problems; and when he decided to do coaching for a living, his sister Nikki asked him if he wanted a golden retriever puppy a friend of hers was trying to sell before leaving town.

Chance wasn't going to take Angie at the start, but Nikki left her with him for a weekend while she flew to Seattle for a reading. Angie convinced him while Nikki was away that they were meant for each other.

Chance pulled up into his sister Nikki's driveway and sat in his car for a moment. He thought back on how, in the past, he was so put off by people who spoke to their dogs as if they were human. Now he was guilty of that and worse. He thought of Angie as his connection to the innocent energy of the universe.

She had taught him how loyal and gentle the universe really was.

Nikki and Angie were standing at the open door and a very excited Angie jumped up into Chance's arms just like in the puppy days.

"Hey, babe, how was your time with your Aunt Nikki?"

Nikki smiled. She never would have thought anything could make her brooding brother so instantly, openly happy.

"Angie was a perfect guest," said Nikki.

Chance, Nikki, and Angie went through the living room out a storm door to the side patio where there was a green wrought-iron table set up for lunch and refreshments.

"I made a fresh batch of iced green tea with mint," said Nikki, "even though I know you're a coffee man."

"The iced tea will be perfect," said Chance. They sat down, with Angie under the table, her head on Chance's lap.

"I enjoyed your reading," Chance said.

"I noticed. You enjoyed it so much you had to leave the room at one point."

"Oh, that. I'd left my phone on vibrate for a case."

"Now it's a 'case.' Before it was just some unresolved issue. Most people worried that you couldn't leave police work behind."

"But not you."

"No, I'm actually happy there's something you can do about your friend's death that's active. You used to tell me when I was younger that love acts the part, and that love is always creative. Whenever I'm feeling out of love I know the way back because of that."

"The way back. Remind me. Remind me of my unforgettable advice that I've forgotten."

"Be active and creative. It's what you always said when I was down."

"Okay, right. Good. That brings me to a question I had for you. Because you're a pre-cog, like in the Tom Cruise movie."

"Whatever."

"I mean you're into all that precognitive, intuitive, non-linear stuff. The fact that we are tuned into an intelligence larger than the one in our minds."

"That's not a belief for me; that's a certainty."

"So I have a dream or memory about an orange tree in Madison's yard."

"She was beautiful."

"What?"

"At the reading. She's so radiant and natural — not all done up like a mankiller, but just naturally full of color. And she obviously connects with you on a very high level."

"You can see that from the front of a room while you're reading?

"We talked after, too, remember."

Chance took a drink of the chilled tea. Maybe he would start giving tea a try. He never remembered it being this good. "I think we've strayed from the subject here," he said, as Nikki was all smiles nibbling at her salad.

"Go on," she said.

"Okay, I'm more of a facts and reality guy. But I respect your thinking and I'm realizing right now that I can solve this case. I think I can find the final missing piece by going somewhere in my mind. Do you know what I mean by that?"

"Absolutely. There is something you know that you don't know you know."

"Exactly! That's exactly how it feels."

"We are taught the most limited ways of thinking, and when the mind opens up, we get a strange feeling."

"Well, this dream is like that."

"And what happens in the dream?"

"Madison is telling me about a calamondin orange in her yard."

"And you think that dream keeps coming back to you because it suggests something about this case you went to Denver for? This suicide?"

"I feel funny saying it, but yes."

"Okay, then follow it. Go more deeply into it."

"How would I do that?"

"Well, I could take you through a couple hours of holotropic breathing exercises right now. That would do it. But I don't think that's your thing."

"You're right. What else could I do instead of whatever that is. Let's say I don't want to hyperventilate, I just want to find an answer."

"I would talk to her."

"To Madison?"

"Yes, to her."

"About?"

"About the tree. Sit with her and have her go back over her whole history with the tree in her yard and just listen and talk."

"I like that better than the breathing thing."

"I thought you would."

68

Madison was not sleeping well. Any little noise had her get out of her bed and pick up her silver and red aluminum softball bat and walk to each dark room in the house.

They were just sending a message, she told herself.

If they had meant to kill her, they would have done it while she was in the car. Or in her room.

She would go back to bed with the bat at her side. She used to sleep with a cricket bat under her bed, but a friend at the health club told her a baseball bat was a better weapon. The black electrical tape wrapped at the bottom of the bat gave her a more secure feeling when she held it. The last thing she wanted was an intruder taking the weapon from her and using it on her.

Each morning, though, was a reward, as if the rising sun was signaling a victory over her fear. Sandy Redfield had said she could stay with him and Ben. That was so tempting, for more reasons than she wanted to admit.

But there was an angry part of her that felt somehow healthy. If they — whoever they were — shot at her car to scare her off the case, she would simply not cooperate. She would not be scared off.

Tonight all the accumulated courage left her in a heartbeat. She heard a scratching outside her living room window, a high-pitched scratch like a thorny branch across a window in a windy storm except that there were no branches at the living room windows. And there was no storm.

Madison grabbed the baseball bat, pulled on a tee shirt, and quietly removed the screen from the inside of her back bedroom window. Her heart was pounding and her hands were shaking, but in no time she was in the back yard, feeling safer than when she was in the house. She stood silently for a moment not daring to move, and then decided to walk quietly into her neighbor's yard and find a roundabout path to the street corner, and then maybe down two blocks to a convenience store to call the police from. The loud scraping scratch on the front window could not have been caused by anything other than a human animal.

As Madison turned away from her house to walk through the damp grass to her neighbor's yard, she felt a sudden impact on her back and then two arms wrapping violently around her from behind. Her bat dropped to the ground.

She had never been this scared in her whole life.

Everything stopped but her heart, which felt like it was going out of control.

Someone was holding her very tight, and then there was a whisper in her ear: "Shhhh. Do not make noise or move." She gulped for air and didn't dare to make a noise. The voice continued, "You are safe. My name is Wu Li."

Her brain fought to make sense of the name Wu Li and who that was, and then she remembered that Chance's beloved trainer was named Wu Li. And after a moment or two of fruitless struggle, the bear hug she was in no longer felt all that violent or aggressive. In a strange way, it was strong but gentle, like her father used to hold her when she was a little girl having a tantrum.

Madison's voice was hoarse, "How do I know you are Wu Li?"

"You will know by my releasing you now."

And he let go of her slowly. Madison lunged for the dropped bat, picked it up by the handle, and faced Wu Li ready to swing.

He stood with his hands folded, almost as if in prayer. He had a smile in his eyes, and he slowly bowed.

"Miss Madison, I have been watching your home. My friend Robert called me from Denver. He has asked me to keep you safe. Tonight someone was at your front window."

"I heard him. Where is he now?"

"He has chosen to leave."

"Did you see him?"

"He was wearing ski mask, but I believe he now has broken ribs. On both sides. He was not walking gracefully when he left. Wu Li requested he not return."

Madison stood and stared at him. Wu Li was not large. But he stood as if he were. She finally sighed and said, "Won't you come inside?"

69

This was Madison's best day in a long time because Chance was back in town and they were going to walk the 3ʳᵈ Street Promenade in Santa Monica at sunset to talk about the case and Chance's meeting with Gibbon in Denver.

Wu Li was no longer a secret guardian, and he had been staying in Madison's living room at night, although as he predicted, no one ever returned to her home.

Yesterday she had finally befriended one of the arson investigators for the Laurel Canyon fire that had started at the Dumar house. Things always seemed to move more quickly when she showed up in person.

"How did you know so fast that this fire was arson?" she had asked fire inspector Duane Raines.

"It's actually very hard for a house to accidentally burn down," he said. "Despite what you think or hear about. Because of oxygen deficiency. There are so many sealed off compartments in a house that it's hard for an internal accidental fire to find enough fuel to do the whole job."

"But Laurel Canyon is pretty isolated," Madison said.

"No, ma'am. Our response time to any Laurel Canyon residence would always be less than eight minutes."

"So how did that one home, the Dumar home, burn down so completely?"

"The arsonist has to provide the fuel. With all the rooms in a home, there just isn't enough oxygen available for a guaranteed total burn-down. So the bad guy has to supply lots of kerosene, or whatever ignitable liquid was used."

"And that guarantees it?"

"Not always. Sometimes, too, like in this case, they knock a lot of drywall out and open big holes in the walls ahead of time."

"That was the part of the report you showed me where the neighbors heard so much banging the night before."

"Right. The cabin was being ventilated from within in case the kerosene wasn't enough."

"Why so thorough?"

"That's what we don't understand. If you want to collect insurance, you don't have to destroy a home that thoroughly."

"And once the fire was started, were there any injuries to anyone?"

"No. Not neighbors, anyway. Not even smoke inhalation. Everyone in the neighborhood got out quickly. We cleared the area. Why are you asking that?"

"We've observed someone we think is connected to the fire still wearing bandages."

"I don't think so. Not from this fire they wouldn't be."

 70

Madison always loved the 3rd Street Promenade. Only pedestrians were allowed to walk the lanes filled with street musicians and magic performers and restaurants and retail shops all along the way. The walk was also refreshing because of the breezes pouring in from the ocean. The promenade was only two blocks from Palisades Park overlooking the Pacific.

Chance and Madison walked slowly as he told his entire Denver experience to her. Madison then talked about her talk with the arson investigator. Then they walked in silence.

"I just love the breezes here," said Madison, breathing deeply as they walked. The sun was going down and the streetlights and store front lights were coming on.

"Santa Monica's a great place," said Chance. "My old partner Rashid used to bug me about my moving here. He was African American, very political, and as close a friend as you'd ever want to have. A truly great cop."

"Why did he bug you about Santa Monica?"

"He said it was guilty of environmental racism."

"What did he mean by that?"

"He found some study that showed that kids in South Central Los Angeles have a third of the lung capacity of kids in Santa Monica."

"Wow."

"Rashid was one of a kind."

"You stay in touch with him?"

"He was killed. Shot by a gang leader. Killed in the line of duty."

Madison didn't know what to say. Chance looked like he was momentarily in a different world. They walked in silence until Chance stopped walking in front of the Broadway Deli at the south end of the promenade.

"Hungry?" said Chance.

"Very."

"I love this place. You? Ever been here?"

"Never."

"The booths are roomy, and there's great matzo-ball soup and very good pizza puttanesca."

"That's an interesting combination of choices."

They went in and found a very roomy booth at the back of the restaurant. Madison ordered a chilled white wine and Chance had a bottle of Dos Equis. Somehow there was a strange sense of privacy inside the chaotic service and the dull background roar of customers.

"I wanted to ask you about something that's been nagging at me," said Chance.

Madison took in a breath and thought of what his question might be. Why am I not married yet? What happened to the fiancé I had just before he started coaching me? What did I think of Sandy Redfield and was I tempted to camp out at his Venice Beach apartment overlooking the water?

Chance adjusted the paper place mat on the table in the booth. It was a map of the California coastline.

"It's about your orange tree," he said.

"You're kidding, right?"

"No, it's going to sound weird, but I think it has something to do with the case."

Madison took a moment. "They wanted to shoot my orange tree but they missed and hit the car windshield instead?"

"You see, I knew this would not be all that clear a topic. I even talked to Nikki about it and she said to talk to you."

"I'm sorry? You had to talk to your sister before asking me about my orange tree?"

"What did you tell me about it, exactly?"

"My calamondin orange."

"Right."

"It died."

"Right. I remember that part."

"And I was lazy and never removed it. Then one morning when I was putting birdseed out in the feeder I noticed little green signs of life in the dead wood. Little funny green sprouts. Fuzzy, too. I thought it might be some kind of parasitical fungus feeding on the rot, just something there to remind me of my negligence and chronic procrastination."

"But it wasn't."

"It wasn't. It was new life. You should see the tree today. I'll show it to you. Would you like to see my tree? I'd love to show you my tree."

Chance said nothing. He was lost in thought.

Madison said, "We could do a biology field trip to my home. I'd give you extra college credits if you can identify the tree we're now talking about."

Chance took a deep drink from his Dos Equis. And stared at Madison. He was looking at her like he was looking through her to something else entirely.

He began tapping the table lightly with the bottom of his bottle.

A bronze-skinned waitress came by with an order pad, "Are you ready to order?"

"Not yet,"said Chance, "Not yet. Not yet."

The waitress said, "Take your time," and walked away.

Chance began shaking his head and saying, "My, my, my…"

"What? What is going on with you?" said Madison.

"My goodness," Chance was nearly shouting.

"That's strong language for you."

"Sorry, I meant to say holy *shit*."

Now Madison was concerned. She'd never seen him this way.

She said, "Can you tell me what you are thinking right now, or should I just call the paramedics?"

Chance said something in a hoarse whisper; and Madison didn't think she heard it, or at least didn't trust what she thought she heard.

"Say that again?"

"Tom Dumar is alive."

"Again?"

"Tom Dumar is freaking *alive.*"

Madison sat in stunned silence. She checked Chance's eyes for signs of mischief. He was serious.

"And by that you mean?" she said.

"By that I mean that Tom Dumar is alive."

"He has come back to life? Like the calamondin?"

"Well in a way. You see, neither of them really died. Both were alive all along; we just *thought* they were dead. That body wasn't him… it was someone, but it wasn't Tom. Maybe it was one of Santa Monica's many homeless people who sleep along the Pacific highway. That doesn't matter for now."

Madison took another sip of her wine and finished the glass. She thought deeply for a minute and then said, "Yes."

"Yes, you can see?"

"Yes. Like Dolly Parton."

"What?"

"Dolly Parton, Bruce Jenner, Meg Ryan…"

"What do you mean?"

"The bandages. On that mystery man. They weren't from a fire at all. Who has bandages on their heads? People getting plastic surgery. Dolly Parton. Bruce Jenner. New faces."

"So if Tom is not dead he would be the man in the bandages."

"Because he got surgery. But I don't understand. How could Mossi's people have made a mistake of that order? I can see getting the suicide wrong, but getting the victim's identity wrong, too?"

"It's not that hard. Unfortunately. I worked a lot of crime scenes and mistakes are easily made, especially when somebody wants you to make them."

"How would that happen?"

"Whoever the body was probably had all of Tom's ID on it, including pictures of Susan and Tom together. The investigators look through the ID and the grieving widow rushes to the scene and they see that it's her — same lady in the photos. She screams when she sees the body and calls his name out and they have to restrain her."

"So by that time identification of the corpse is the last thing on their minds."

"Right. Cops and CSI are fallible human beings and their minds move quickly to the next task at hand. Identification of the body would no longer be an issue. They would move on now to whether this gunshot wound is close range enough to be consistent with suicide, and you always just tend to see what you believe."

"You see what you believe," said Madison.

"You do!" said Chance who took a moment to think further. "The body would also have his office keys in his pocket, the door was locked and whoever found him unlocked the door and went in, finding him dead, no signs of forced entry. It was very easy to jump to the conclusion he locked himself in his office and killed himself."

"Do we *all* see what we believe?"

"Right. We all do. Cops are no different. If we believe we are seeing the aftermath of that woman's husband's suicide, we can close this thing quickly and get on with our under-staffed case loads."

"Wouldn't Mossi have even looked into it to verify the belief?"

"Sure. He interviews her and some other people. Finds out Tom was upside down in a bunch of real estate deals, depressed, a victim of the recession. Whatever. But it all fits."

"How could Mossi have done it differently, so that he wasn't so sure of what was untrue?"

"When you get to a crime scene," and here Chance paused to take another swallow of Dos Equis because he could now see that this applied everywhere in life ... "you need to keep an open mind, sit back and listen, stop trying to *tell the story* and listen to what you are being told. Holds true for coaching people, too."

"And this story looked true because Tom Dumar made it look true."

Chance nodded yes. "Tom must have noticed that Gibbon was really attracted to his wife so he asked himself how he could use that weakness in Gibbon to solve everything."

"But how could you have missed all this as his coach?"

Chance smiled and raised his empty Dos Equis bottle up for the waitress to see. When she arrived at the table he said, "Two more."

Madison said, "You're having two more beers?"

The waitress stopped and looked at Chance.

"No, of course not, I meant a beer for me and a wine for you."

"How did you know I wanted another wine?"

"Don't you?"

"That's beside the point."

Chance didn't know what to say.

Madison said, "Are you like my daddy saying 'bring the little girl another glass of milk?'"

"Would you like another glass of wine?"

"Yes."

Chance sighed and looked at the waitress who smiled and left.

"So what do we do now?" said Madison.

"When the drinks get here, we tell her what we want for dinner."

"No, I meant on this case."

"We look at the autopsy photos of Tom Dumar."

"Will Sergeant Mossi let you do that?"

"He doesn't really have a choice. The freedom of information act gives us access to the medical examiner's full files. And yes, he will let us do that."

"And what about my other question?"

"What was that?"

"How you could have missed this as Tom's coach. I'm worried now that you're missing things in me."

"I probably am! But now that I think about it, there was a lot of anger in Tom about Gibbon. And Tom always had a thing about revenge. It always fascinated him. His favorite movies were about revenge."

"Like what movies?"

"Like *One-Eyed Jacks* with Marlon Brando. Tom had seen that movie about twenty times, he said."

"Tom must have had his ego really wounded by Gibbon."

"He did. I worked with him a lot on that. Obviously not enough."

"Well, I'm just kidding about you missing things. I think you're a great coach."

"Thank you."

"What would you want for Tom right now? If you were still coaching him?"

"You mean something that would wake him up? Enlighten him to live at his next level of consciousness?"

"Right."

"Prison."

● ● ● 71 ● ● ●

Chance camped his car out across the street from Susan Dumar's sister's house for two hours before he saw Susan walk to the road and stand there, as if waiting to be picked up.

He drove up in his open MG and called out cheerfully, "Susan! Ride with me! I'll bring you right back. I have news."

Susan looked down the street nervously and then walked up to Chance's car.

"Hello Robert. I'm getting picked up in a few minutes by a friend."

"That's okay, I'll get you right back. We need to talk. It's about Tom."

Susan hesitated, trying to read Chance's face, but he was relaxed and cheerful, so she got in.

Chance said, "Shoreline Park is just a few blocks down. Right? Let's go there and talk and I'll have you back here in no time. Need to call someone?"

"No, not yet. Let's just go."

Chance and Susan drove about five blocks through the quiet Santa Barbara neighborhood and parked on the street at the entrance to Shoreline Park. Susan used to go often to this park with her sister. It offered fabulous views of the harbor, the islands, and the mountains.

Chance walked down some narrow wooden stairs to the beach tidal pool area. Susan followed reluctantly. In happier times she and her sister and little niece would sometimes see dolphins skimming the surface from this viewpoint. Today, her mind was preoccupied.

Two people were there walking their dogs past the tidal pool, and Chance and Susan found a circular wooden bench to sit on.

Susan checked her cell phone screen and then looked up at Chance and tried to smile.

"How have you been, Robert? I haven't heard from you. You look good. You look fit as always."

"Traveling a bit and I'm doing well. But what about you? I'm concerned about you Susan, you know, first Tom and then the fire."

"I'm okay. I have my moments. I'm sure you understand. Tom and I were together for twelve years."

"Yes. I know. When you say you have your moments, tell me what those moments are like. I mean, it would help to talk about it, right?"

Susan and Chance sat and adjusted themselves on the on the bench so they could see each other better. A young woman in coveralls went by walking a beige and brown Jack Russell terrier she was calling "Latte." The dog looked like he wanted to jump more than walk. She also had a little boy with her who had on a tiny camouflage military outfit.

Chance nodded toward the boy and said to Susan, "That camouflage is cute, but we used to tell parents not to buy that kind of clothing."

"When you were a policeman?"

"Yes."

"Why was that?"

"If a child gets lost, especially in a wooded area, and they're wearing camouflage, they are very hard to see."

"Which is the whole point of camouflage, I suppose."

"Yes it is. It's a deliberate attempt to become hard to locate."

Susan watched the boy, the terrier, and the mom walk away. She wasn't interested in continuing this line of conversation. Chance kept looking at her in a friendly, inviting way.

"Want to talk about all these stresses we've been through?" said Chance.

"I don't need to talk about it Robert. You said you had some news. And I do have to get back pretty quick—not that it isn't wonderful to see you."

"You just said you had your moments, and I wondered what those moments were like."

Susan sighed. "You know what grief does. I don't have to go into it."

"I do know what grief is like."

"I'm sure you do."

"Grief usually involves a loss, though."

Susan stopped looking around and focused on Chance.

"And what is that supposed to mean?"

"I'm just thinking back on the history of grief."

"Yes?"

"And, at least in this culture, it's traditionally connected with losing someone. Someone dying or disappearing. Maybe even a child going into the woods in a camouflage suit and never being found. There would be grief in that. But it's always a loss that triggers it, don't you agree?"

"Robert, I don't know what you're trying to do right now. Maybe this is one of your coaching tricks where you try to break the paradigm I'm in, like Tom used to say you did with him…."

"No, no. I don't want to break the paradigm you are in. Not at all. I just want to get a better picture of it. A more accurate one than I had at the beginning."

"And?"

"Because, at the start, I believed the paradigm that you presented to me. And if I had early doubts about the suicide, I never doubted that Tom was dead."

"No one did."

"Well now I don't know. So maybe you can introduce me to the new paradigm."

Susan said nothing. She pulled her phone out of her purse and checked the screen for messages. She brushed her hair back and sighed and looked around the park.

Chance said, "I know that this must be awkward for you Susan."

"Only because you're not making sense. And frankly you're scaring me."

"Well, let me just give you the news then."

"Good, give me the news; then I have to get back."

"Based on some research I've done, and interesting people I met during my travels, it now looks like Tom didn't die after all. I thought you'd be glad to hear that."

Susan was quiet. Then she said, "Have you based this whole theory on that suicide note that was 'you and I' instead of 'you and me'?"

"No, I'm way past that, Susan. Although we weren't wrong about that note. It wasn't written by Tom. I talked to the person who wrote it."

Susan said nothing. She studied her shoes and shook her head.

Chance said, "Look… I'm not a cop anymore, Susan. You know that. Tom was my coaching client and he had become my friend…"

"I don't know what you're doing, but I do have to get back."

"And because I'm not with law enforcement, my interest isn't in justice or punishment for anyone, because I'm going to leave that to others. My interest is in simple resolution. I hate to have a client just up and leave without completing the work. So I knew you'd be the one to get that message to Tom for me."

Susan stood up and brushed her jeans and began walking away. Chance fell in beside her.

"So wherever you and Tom are headed, please tell him he needs a final session first. There are a lot of things I obviously left out of our coaching together."

"You're playing some kind of sick mind game based on some theory you have. You're trying to get me to say something."

"I don't need you to say anything, Susan. It's all filled in. All the blanks. I spent some time with your other boyfriend Glen Gibbon in Denver. Of course you knew he was Brock Young now. It's amazing how many changes have been put in motion by this whole thing. But one thing that never changes is that no one ever gets away with anything. Ever notice that? Ever. There is no such thing as something for nothing. You and Tom will notice that. Maybe that's all the coaching Tom will need is that final noticing. The mind thinks it can get something for nothing, and it can't."

"Why are you even talking to me if you think you know all this? Is this some kind of attempted set up?"

"Oh, no. I just wanted to put my two cents in right at the end here. We're all so busy these days, aren't we? We hardly ever find the time to go to a park like this and just talk."

"So you're not trying to get me on tape."

"No, no. That's not necessary. You guys are done, tapes or not."

"What exactly did you think this conversation with me would achieve?"

"I don't know. Maybe speed the process up a little."

Susan was walking at a faster pace now and finally Chance just let her go. She was only a few blocks from her sister's house, and she looked like a race walker striding and pumping down the road. He took a slow walk back to his car and then drove a wide circular route back to Susan's sister's neighborhood in time to see her get into an orange van that sped off.

As he drove home he decided to take a scenic road and drive along the ocean for a while. He realized that a few years ago he would have frantically jumped into action, arranging arrests, stings, and take downs; but something in him now was content to have the way of the universe achieve its own reckoning.

He liked the idea that Mossi could do his thing now without Chance taking all the credit. Chance didn't really even need to see Tom again. Let's just say that going into prison with unfinished plastic surgery would be like a final coaching session. Pretty harsh coaching, but perfect for Tom right now.

Something for nothing.

It never works.

In fact, it's worse than that. It always blows up. It always explodes in your face. Chance recalled the character in the Nabokov story that blew his hand off trying to invent antimatter. Something for nothing. All the same foolish mission.

In all his years as a cop, Chance noticed that no one ever really got away with anything. Because wherever they ran to, they themselves would be there—even if their names had changed. It was the same sad person, now psychologically worse off than ever.

Something for nothing was the road to hell.

Chance was reminded of a business coaching client of his who was always seeking "passive income." It was the same futile thing. The client had spent more fruitless, frustrating hours working on his "passive income" schemes than he ever spent just serving people and collecting payment.

There *is* no passive income.

And there is no such reality as something for nothing.

Chance drove on. He put in his old Eagles CD of songs he'd loved since high school and allowed himself a peaceful, easy feeling as he drove along the ocean highway. Something wonderful was happening. Something free and lighthearted had begun to grow in Chance's world, and he couldn't define it but he liked how it felt.

72

At first, Mossi wasn't buying it. Chance sat in a chair in front of Mossi's desk laying out the whole case to him as the sergeant kept shaking his head and giving Chance a pitying, tight-lipped smile. Poor man. Wants to be a cop again. Out of touch with reality.

"Why would they burn the cabin down like that?" said Mossi.

"To get rid of evidence, the two computers, and to eliminate anything, like toothbrushes, combs, that would have Tom's DNA."

Mossi laughed. "We could get his DNA from his parents. They're still alive. They went to the funeral."

"Step parents."

"Oh, okay."

Mossi got up and walked to his window. He said, "But what were they thinking? That we would do a DNA match off the corpse we found to see if it was Tom? You already said we were set up by them to not even look into that."

"You know, it's hard to demand logical sequences from the criminal mind. You know that better than anyone. Crime happens after a breakdown in the mind. The whole emotional system is dysfunctional when crime happens so it won't always give you excellent logic. And then again I'm just guessing at what happened."

"You really are. Prints of the body would be taken at the time of the autopsy and ran through AFIS. If Tom himself had a clean criminal history, no prints would be on file to compare against. But if the deceased had a criminal history, they would have caught the switch."

"So maybe the deceased didn't. A lot of younger homeless men do not have fingerprints on record. But I'm leaving the investigation up to you, because I know you'll do it right."

"Okay. But let's say you were still on the job here. What would your next action be?"

"Look at the medical examiner's photos. You and I could do that now. I knew my client. I'll know if it's him."

"The wife knew it was him at the scene. She didn't look like she was faking her reaction to the sight of the body."

"Susan has talent."

"So you say."

"Besides, the sight of a body, any body, with a gunshot to the head, probably causes a reaction you don't have to fake, right?"

"Maybe not."

73

Gibbon had gone straight to bed after Chance's visit and stayed there for two days trying not to call Susan and warn her that it was over. Part of him wanted to talk to her, but the other part of him hated her now almost as much as he hated life itself.

He would not call.

He would sleep just a bit more and then leave town. Where would he go? He no longer cared.

Now Gibbon was finding it hard to figure out how long he had slept. He'd begun to hear strange noises, maybe from dreams but maybe not. Long low notes played by a bow on a bass violin.

He felt his left arm get tingly like it was on fire, and then it went completely numb. He sat up in bed. The pressure on his chest made it almost impossible to breathe, and then the burning started. It was like when he was in high school when his so-called friends at church camp had made him eat a quart of hot green chili peppers.

It was unbearable.

He got out of bed, using his one good arm to push himself up and around to the floor. He had to get help. He had to call 911 but his cell phone wouldn't cooperate. His hand was dripping with sweat and shaking so badly that his attempts at 911 kept popping up to the screen as 991 and 999 and then 666.

The wet phone was thrown at the wall.

He got to his closet and used one arm to pull a pale green Guayabera shirt off the hanger. He managed to get the unbuttoned shirt on so he was now in bare feet, bright blue boxer shorts with white Dodger logos on them, and a green Mexican wedding shirt that felt like it was on inside out.

He made it out into the hall and walked up to the elevator. It took the doors forever to open, and once he got inside he dropped immediately to the floor and tried but couldn't get up.

The elevator wasn't moving.

This is how it would end.

A nobody found curled up in a large, unmoving cube of empty space.

But now the floor was moving down. The elevator's motion was starting to make Gibbon feel nauseous.

He didn't know if a few minutes or an hour had passed but a middle-aged woman who looked like an Indian chief was staring at him, her face next to his, yelling, "Mr. Young! Mr. Young!"

Who in the world was Mr. Young?

Paramedics were sitting next to him now. Now he was on a cot in a vehicle that was moving very fast as a distant siren kept sounding. One female paramedic, a young woman who looked like his daughter Carrie, only with dark hair, was holding his two prescription bottles in his face.

"How many?" she kept saying to him but he couldn't make his mouth move. His lips felt like they had novocaine in them. He wanted to form the words *"side effects include"* but couldn't. His eyes were burning and people were multiplying in his vision. One paramedic became identical twins right before his eyes.

If I were any happier I'd have to be twins.

Who had he said that to? Where was he going? Why would Susan do all this? He could see her changing her mind, but why would she do all *this*?

■ ■ ■

Brock Young was pronounced dead on arrival at Exempla St. Joseph Hospital in Denver at 11:27 a.m. that day.

The hospital administration was unable to find any next of kin, and when they turned their report over to the coroner's office it was determined that Young's identification was false.

His body was kept under "John Doe AKA Brock Young" pending further investigation.

 **74**

Sandy Redfield had called Madison twice while she was at the Promenade deli with Chance. On her way home she listened to his voicemail.

"I've got some work... *possible* work for you," he said. "Mr. Boston has given me a budget because of my case load, and I get to sub out some work if I want. It's a nice budget, and I have two cases right now that have a lot of internet stuff that I don't have time for. I'd like to try you out as an assistant to me, just for these two cases. If you want the work call me."

Madison clicked her phone closed and let herself just relax. Even though it was the black of night she felt like she was giving off soft beams of sunlight.

She realized that ever since she put her hopes and dreams for abundance away she had begun attracting money. Left and right. Not only for her internet marketing consulting—London was only a week away—but also now for investigation work, her new love.

But was she actually *attracting* money? What would Robert say?

You are earning it, he would say. You are taking the *actions* that make it happen. He'd say it was cause and effect.

She was the cause. Money was the effect. She remembered one of her coaching sessions with Robert and how it ended with him saying, "I want you to always see yourself as the cause in your life, not the effect. I'd like you to even consider getting a license plate for your car that says CAUSE on it."

She felt warm at the thought.

75

Chance and his frisky dog Angie were taking a long walk along the beach when Mossi called him with news of the arrests. Tom and Susan Dumar were arrested together in Nogales, Arizona, three days after Glen Gibbon's body was accurately identified in Denver.

Tom Dumar was no longer wearing bandages on his face where the plastic surgery had been performed, but he was wearing a medical corset over heavily bandaged ribs on both sides. When Chance heard about the broken ribs he knew it was the work of Wu Li. Tom had often told him he wanted to give Wu Li a try, and now he had.

Chance wasn't surprised when he heard all this news. After he and Mossi studied the autopsy photos and saw that the body was not Tom's, the wheels of Mossi's investigative machine had gone into overdrive.

He knew that when Susan Dumar had said she might go to Canada, it probably meant the opposite direction. Like Mexico. Which is where the border town of Nogales was leading.

Chance and Mossi agreed to have coffee someday soon and compare notes on this case and others.

Chance and his dog had started at the pier and wandered north along the shoreline. The sun kept burning through the chilly winds. Angie was chasing the sandpipers into the water and now brought Chance a stick of glistening driftwood to throw to her. She knew he was always happier when they both had something to play with.

Chance had his cell phone in his jeans pocket, which was unusual for him. He wasn't much of a cell phone guy. But today he kept reaching down to feel if it was still there. It was. And then he threw the piece of driftwood as far as he could and admired Angie's speed in chasing it down.

He pulled his phone from his pocket and punched in Madison's number. She answered right away.

"This is Madison."

"This is Robert Chance."

"Yes, I know who you are."

"Two days from now... actually two nights... there's a kind of moonlight thing...." and Chance suddenly couldn't find the words he wanted to say.

"A kind of moonlight thing?"

"No, no. A client of mine is having a moonlight dance... a party or a gathering... get-together in Marina del Rey by the water two nights from now."

"Sounds nice."

"And he asked me to come and he said to bring a guest or a date...and..."

"And what?"

Chance pulled the stick out of Angie's mouth and threw it even farther this time.

"So I thought... if you're not busy, you might go."

"You thought I might go? Why would I go?"

"You know what I mean. You might go with me."

"To dance?"

"You wouldn't have to dance. If you didn't want to."

"But I love dancing."

"Then you could dance."

"With you?"

"I would hope for that, being that you were my guest... my, well, date. Given that I was the one who brought you."

"You're going to bring me?"

Chance couldn't figure out why this was so hard. Finally

he decided to simplify things: "May I pick you up at seven and take you there?"

"That would be wonderful."

Chance smiled at the tail wagging on Angie and said goodbye. Madison said goodbye, too.

He and Angie walked more lightheartedly now. The stick sailed out across the wave-soaked sand, and the stick came racing back in the mouth of a true retriever. Could there be a prettier dog in all the world? Could there be a more beautiful ocean to be walking along?

Anywhere in the universe?

Coming soon....

A CRIME OF
GENIUS

a Robert Chance mystery

STEVE CHANDLER

Also by Steve Chandler

RelationShift (with Michael Bassoff)
100 Ways to Motivate Yourself
Reinventing Yourself
17 Lies That Are Holding You Back
50 Ways to Create Great Relationships
100 Ways to Create Wealth (with Sam Beckford)
The Small Business Millionaire (with Sam Beckford)
9 Lies that are Holding Your Business Back (with Sam Beckford)
Business Coaching (with Sam Beckford)
How to Get Clients
Two Guys Read Moby Dick (with Terrence N. Hill)
Two Guys Read the Obituaries (with Terrence N. Hill)
Two Guys Read Jane Austen (with Terrence N. Hill)
The Hands-off Manager (with Duane Black)
The Story of You
100 Ways to Motivate Others (with Scott Richardson)
10 Commitments to Your Success
The Joy of Selling
Fearless
Shift Your Mind: Shift the World

About the Author

Steve Chandler is the author of numerous books. He is a business coach and public speaker who lives with his wife Kathy and dog Jimmy in Arizona.

Steve also heads up the world mastermind success coaching group called Club Fearless (www.clubfearless.net.) You can reach the author at www.stevechandler.com.